Jump in Jill

by

Gillian Martell

Copyright © Gillian Martell 2008

For Barbara, who took me seriously
and put her metaphorical money where my mouth was.

INTRODUCTION

My cousin, Susan, and I were born in the reign of Edward VIII which we always felt to be quite a distinction, and we grew up together which made life twice as much fun. There were three weeks and two days between us, and three weeks and one day whenever it wasn't a leap year. Thus, although we were pre-war babies, our clearer memories took place during the war. In one way it is good to grow up in times of austerity as it makes the special occasions and special treats stand out in glittering clarity.

For my cousin and me the special treat was always to be taken to lunch at the Trocadero in London. This vast palace was to us the Ritz, Claridges and possibly Buckingham Palace rolled in to one and I was astonished to learn in later life that it was in reality nothing more than a glorified Lyon's Corner House. However, the manners and customs obtaining there were certainly those of the big hotels and we were made to feel very important by their treatment of us.

To begin with, there was a cloakroom where a lady was stationed solely in order to take charge of our coats and hats, which we handed over on entering. We were then revealed in all the glory of our best clothes – I particularly remember an occasion when Susan and I were clad identically in royal blue pleated skirts with bright yellow fluffy jumpers and mine was distinguished from hers by the addition of a blue brooch of my mother's, which exactly matched my skirt. We proceeded to the bar, where we were handed our very special cocktails that we firmly believed had been devised specifically for us. After sipping these down in a ladylike manner, possibly with the aid of a straw if such a thing were available – and it often was in this magnificent refuge from the austerities of our normal lives – we then went in to dine.

The dining area was vast – even to adult eyes I believe – sombre-coloured with heavy furniture and plenty of space between tables. We would wend our way, as seasoned habitués, to our particular table, which I suppose had been reserved for us, but we imagined that nobody else ever sat there, or at least never if they knew we were in town. There we were joined by 'our' waiter, whom we familiarly called 'Sandra' (or was it 'Zandra'?). He was a short, plump, middle aged man with a warm smile and he treated us with familiarity seasoned with a becoming deference, and relayed the menu to us with recommendations, whilst also drawing to our attention any other notables currently dining with us. He must have been a refugee of some kind, I think. His accent we just accepted. It was part of his exciting 'waiteryness'. I mean, you don't want to be called Madam in everyday accents do you? I have no idea of his nationality – he certainly wasn't French and obviously not German. Hungarian perhaps? Czech? Polish? He was just 'Sandra', and our friend.

On one very memorable occasion I was lunching there without my aunt and cousin, just with my mother. This was later in the war and Sandra was able to point out several celebrities in uniform, amongst whom were quite a few Americans. One name seemed to cause my Mother great excitement but I don't think I paid a great deal of heed as I was concentrating on my food. I was rather fond of food even in those days and liked to pay it the respect of close attention. We finished our meal and wanted to leave the building by way of the large revolving doors in the entrance hall. As we approached them a party of people made their exit and left them spinning with what I felt was alarming speed. I was an extremely timid child with an over developed awareness of danger and liked to play it safe at all times. And here I was deprived of the moral support of my bolder cousin, with my Mother urging me to step into these doors which were definitely still in motion. I wasn't about to go in there until they had finally come to a full stop. People had now come up behind us and were forming a polite queue. My Mother renewed her embarrassed exhortations. I may have been timid but I was also stubborn, especially in support of my own safety, and I refused to budge. Then a voice behind me encouraged "Jump in Jill", and I was aware of my Mother apologising for me in a very flustered way as the voice repeated its slogan kindly "Jump in Jill". I should like to record that I instantly took the plunge but I'm afraid that I just subsided in tears, startled by the fact that this tall military gentleman apparently knew my name and had actually addressed me in person, forgetting that my Mother had been repeating my name plaintively as he approached. The party laughed and left the building and so did my Mother and I, after she had eventually calmed me down.

It was only later, as she relayed the story to everyone we met, that I was brought to realise that my friendly American adviser was none other than James Stewart, the Hollywood star. And much later indeed that I became proud, instead of ashamed, of the story as I saw more films and came to revere James Stewart as my very favourite film actor. In retrospect I saw his advice to me as urging me to "Jump in" to the uncertain world of the theatre, despite my timid nature. And I see it now as a sign that I should "Jump in" to the world of writing, to round off my life.

So here goes ....

SCHOOL

Some explanation of the following piece is due. I felt I should include something about my schooldays but found my memory somewhat hazy. Whilst researching amongst the collection of pieces and fragments of paper which my Mother conscientiously preserved, and I have inherited, I came across this scurrilous exercise written by me, aged fourteen. I decided to include it as being at least authentic.

"Snaz", I should explain, was in reality Sister Athanasie, a sister of the order of "Les Soeurs du Saint Esprit", a Breton order in whose Convent of the Holy Ghost Bedford I gained my education. During the war we naturally lost contact with the Mother House and made up the deficiency with Irish nuns and some lay teachers. Due to the paucity of teacher trained religieuses "Snaz" was compelled to teach. It should never have been allowed – for her own sake. We treated her mercilessly. Looking back I see her as a gallant little figure with her squint, her small stature, and her ever hopeful tenacity.

~~~~~~~~~~~~~~~~~~~~~~~~~~~~~

The arrival of the French lesson is the signal for an outburst of chatter and discussion. In a few minutes the classroom is in a state of amiable chaos and the clatter of desks and the chatter of voices effectively drown the entrance of the French teacher who answers to the name of Snaz. She is so small and always enters so quietly that nobody ever sees her. After contemplating the scene in bewilderment for a few seconds she turns and goes out, making more noise than when she came in. A few girls remark her exit, but most of the class have remained happily oblivious of her presence, and the noise does not lessen. Indeed it redoubles, for the class is now in its stride. This is Snaz's cue. She makes another and louder entrance, of the kind that cannot but be noticed. Those girls who have in their travels reached the other side of the room begin to make their adieus but otherwise there is no marked change in the behaviour of the class. By now some minutes have passed. Snaz is still standing just inside the door, gazing with a rather defeatist air at the back view of the girls who will next year belong to the sixth form. These are the girls who must pass their exam In French at the end of this year; and not only pass but pass well. And the task of bringing this unlikely result about has fallen to her. She has been teaching them now for over a year. Or has she? She wasn't quite sure. She has a horrible suspicion that perhaps she hasn't. She has meant to of course, but somehow when one gets among this crowd of noisy young school girls, it is difficult to do what one intends. They have a way of conducting the lesson themselves, and their programme doesn't really agree with her recollections of her own schooldays. No, she definitely hasn't taught them. She has conscientiously attempted to go through her syllabus, but it is very much to be doubted that she has actually taught them anything. Rather apologetically she ventures to speak.

"Well, really!"

This witty observation does not produce the desired effect; it is not at all encouraging. Perhaps this is because she has uttered the self-same observation every day for over a year and it is "not as sweet now as it was before." She tries again.

"Well!" (She has a trick of beginning most of her sentences with 'well', which is foolish because it is obviously not well.)

"Well, I did not expect fifth form girls to behave like this." The class look vaguely affronted. Where she gets her over-rated notions as to the behaviour of fifth forms, nobody knows. It is certain that she has never met a class that behaved in the approved manner. It must be supposed that she read about it when she was young. She has decided to brazen it out. She advances to the desk and climbs into it. Then she arranges her books in a circle all round her. Thus fortified she takes courage and stands up erect. She has now gained the half-amused attention of the class. They are all more or less sitting down, though not in the right places.

"Good morning sister." (Though it is now nearly lunch-time.) Pause, while Snaz folds her arms. She is a truly impressive sight, standing there with one eye looking east and the other looking west, the while she ejaculates, "Well!"

She gives a detailed description of the various books she wishes them to take, then with an air of making an astonishing statement; she says "Now", (a variant on her customary 'well'.)

"Now we are going to prepare......." Pause to regain the attention of the class. "We are going to prepare our homework." The class have other ideas about this. Some are doing Maths, some making out hockey lists, others merely reading. The better behaved members of the class go to sleep, but politely refrain from snoring. Maureen alone remains attentive for her special mission in life is to make helpful suggestions when Snaz finds the interest of the class rather lacking, and to misunderstand her every few minutes. Perhaps Anne too is attending, for every day for over a year she is called upon to read the passage to be translated. Snaz gives the number of the page in French. After a good deal of time everybody appears to have found it.

"Voulez-vous lire, Anne Cookesley?" Anne commences. Pause while everybody asks everybody else what page it is. Anne scrambles through a paragraph. It does not matter how she reads as Snaz is rather deaf. Dawn, who sits behind her, prepares for her turn. Nobody else bothers. Snaz cannot see further than the second bench.

"Voulez-vous lire, Dawn Sharpe?"

"Please sister, I can't. I've got a cold." She is allowed to sit down again. Delighted, the rest of the second row, when called upon, inform sister in varying tones of affliction that they too have bad colds, isn't it sad. Maureen starts a volley of apologetic sneezes, someone else develops an 'acking cough. Thirty two handkerchiefs are sadly produced. Pause for breakdown. Mary Savory kindly assists Jill to put her handkerchief back in her knickers. At a word of command all handkerchiefs disappear and the class turns to smile wearily at Snaz once more. Visibly shaken she finishes the reading herself. Then she announces that she is going to translate. The girls who are doing maths put down their books and wake up their neighbours who sleep. All the girls, except Mary, who never does her homework, produce notebooks and take down the translation, considerably hampered by the fact that

Snaz stops every few minutes to write upon the blackboard a list of words, none of which appear to have any connection with the passage in hand. The girls take the opportunity to doze off for a short while. When the translating is over each girl returns to her former occupation and Snaz in her turn produces a notebook. She has not the faintest idea what to do next, so she waves the book about menacingly, threatening to write down the name of any girl who misbehaves. Why she should do this, nobody knows, for she never reports anyone. Perhaps it comforts her to read them over in her spare time, or perhaps she is making a collection. If she is, she will not get very far as she usually only scribbles wildly with her fingers making no pretence of using a pencil. Somebody suggested it one day, but she didn't catch on.

Several attempts have been made during the lesson to tell her that the bell has gone, but she is at least wise enough to ignore these. AT LAST the bell really does go and she is loudly and incessantly informed of the fact by a class which has shut its books with an air of finality. She is well trained. She does not attempt, as other mistresses would do, to finish her sentence. She shuts her mouth as abruptly as the class have shut their books, and gathering her books departs muttering a vague benediction. The class rise, and for the benefit of the next mistress who is waiting to come in, chorus sweetly and fervently,

"Good morning and thank you sister." Thus endeth the French lesson.

C'est amusant, n'est-ce pas?

LETTER TO MY PARENTS

Dear Mummy and Daddy,

I have to write this letter to you jointly because you were never really happy being separated. You were the most loving and mutually supportive pair of people I ever knew. I always feel very selfish and slightly guilty that I was your only child and so the most direct beneficiary of so much love and attention. But not the sole beneficiary by a long way. All my cousins and my early friends and any stray children who came your way, they all remember you now and often with gratitude and affection. I am glad that I was at least able to provide you with two grand-children to make up for all those other children you should have had and didn't. You had never been very strong Mummy – a result of having been a seven-month child, born in 1910, weighing a little over two pounds and abandoned by the doctor who is reputed to have remarked (though not to Granny) "Drown the little rat"! But what am I saying? Of course you were stronger in spirit or you would never have survived, thanks to the care of the midwife, wonderful Auntie Nan (a courtesy title) who brought all your generation, and a great many of mine, into the world. She was a Christian Scientist and she treated you like a new born lamb: constantly changing hot-water bottles round you as you lay in front of the fire and feeding you with a fountain pen filler – or that's the legend anyway. But you had a sickly child hood and, though you gave birth to me with Auntie Nan's help without too much trouble, you later had a miscarriage which left you rather delicate again. And then came the war with all its uncertainties. My father was in the army for the duration and when he was finally demobbed I was already nine and you never did get round to having another child. Perhaps I was too demanding or perhaps I just totally put you off the idea of having children altogether.

And you know, my darlings, it was a bit unthinking of you to have given me such a solid basis of love and security to my life. You knew I was going to be a great artist and you deprived me of the difficult and unhappy childhood which would have developed my character and understanding and honed my latent talents. I know you were very proud of me, but think what a genius I could have been had you understood your parental obligations a little better!

I miss you both very much but I am glad that you were both spared a lengthy period of the miseries attendant on geriatric illnesses and decline. You, Daddy, always said that you would like to go as you father had, in your sleep, having a rest in your favourite chair after lunch. And I'm sure God loved you very much because that is exactly what happened. A fearful shock for us, of course, but good for you as you would have hated being looked after as an invalid by us – you the supreme carer for others would have hated to have others care for you. And you, Mummy. I knew you would not linger all that long after him, even though I tried to care for you in the manner to which he had accustomed you. Your brain tumour, which turned you abruptly from a pretty good Times Crossword expert to someone who couldn't find her way to the bathroom, did not allow you to remain for more that two or three months in that state.

And you achieved a certain contentment and even made us laugh tenderly with your strange obsession with George Aligayah, then only a voice on the radio from South Africa, and your fantasies about the war and meeting the Queen in the air-raid shelter. I still fondly remember you asking me to warn Betty Boothroyd that her carriage was going to be blown up on the way to the House – I think you imagined she went in a golden coach. And I remember with a certain embarrassment how you sat in a roomful of inmates of the respite care home and suddenly remarked "What do we think about the Germans?", and then – dear, erstwhile refined and proper you - produced a really vulgar raspberry.

But you are both at peace now.

I always think of life as a game of Snakes and Ladders, and I have now got you both safely Home: no more Snakes to slide down. You both climbed your ladders in your steady, un-assuming, middle-class way but your ladders were side by side and you always held hands. And you accepted the snakes in your life with dignity and persevered, still hand in hand.

You would be proud of your grand-children now – the secure world you created has been handed down and though the dice seem somewhat loaded these days they are facing their own snakes and ladders with confidence.

Thank you both for being you. I don't mind not being a genius – honestly!

Your loving daughter,

                Gill

GRANDPA GARNER

Perhaps it was cheating to take a picture as my chosen object to my writing class - *'Bring in an object, describe it and its significance to you'* - because it had such a direct significance. But at least it wasn't a photograph.

The picture is a caricature – no not that, because caricatures are distorted and often cruel – it's a loving portrait of my Grandfather and it is more exactly like him that any photograph. He is seen in his blue Sunday suit counting a pile of money which is labelled "The Garner Store". He was the treasurer of the P.C.C. at All Saints Church, Kempston – a church warden too – for many years before my father took over the job.

The drawing is by Eric Volz, always known familiarly as Sammy Volz, for years the Art Master at Bedford Modern School. I think he labelled it the Garner Store because of the simple pride and enjoyment which is there in my Grandfather's smile in the picture. The smile records the fact of a job well done, not that the money was his. It is that smile of his that I will always remember. He was a very simple man, my grandfather: a farmer by trade and by every inclination. He could lean on a gate and discuss a cow with a fellow farmer for hours, in accents reminiscent of those Bernard Miles used in his rural monologues. When I say discuss, I do not mean anything lively. In fact, it always reminds me of a sketch we did in one of our 'concerts'. Three old men sit round a table with tankards of beer. Nothing is said but eventually an off-stage "Moo" is heard. Silence. Then one says,

"That be Farmer Giles' cow!"

More silence and some contemplative drinking. Then a second one says,

"That b'aint Farmer Giles' cow"

Silence again. Then the third man finishes his drink, slowly gets up and says,

"I ain't come 'ere to listen to no ruddy argument". Whereupon he leaves. This just about illustrates the pace of life and depth of thought of my grandfather. I don't mean to belittle the profundity of his mental processes, I just mean that much time and care was taken over them, and the answers he came up with were simple and straightforward.

He was a dairy farmer principally, but farming was always a bit mixed in those days and there were some pigs, some horses, some crops and, of course, hens everywhere. The hens were mainly my grandmother's concern, straying organically all over the farmyard and leaving their little free-range products in hedges and behind barns, all to provide us children with a ready made game of 'hunt the thimble'.

Once, Grandpa put my cousin and me in charge of a new-born calf each. We had to feed them with bottles first and then with buckets. We called them 'Black Nose' and 'Pink Nose' respectively because Grandpa had said we mustn't give them proper names as we might then get too possessively fond of them and they had to join the herd. His cows all had names though, and he loved them all. He always called his bull 'The Old Boy' and I sensed he felt a keen kinship with him. Grandpa had four daughters and just the one son, quiet and even tempered like himself, so the house was full of female bustle and chatter. But like the 'Old Boy' with his herd of cows, from which he lived withdrawn and solitary until needed, Grandpa knew that he was the king-pin around which everything revolved.

He had a very sweet nature and he loved us all with great pride and no discrimination. He normally wore an old light brown overall-type coat and the pockets of this were unsewn on one side at the top so that there was a way through to his jacket pockets underneath. He had one very clever trick which occurred around Christmas time. We were invited to feel in his overall pocket, which proved to be empty. After a bit of distracting banter we were invited to feel again, but deeper. By this time, to our amazement, we would discover a pair of fur gloves, just our size and handy for the coming winter.

I amused him with my intellectual and theatrical pretensions, and he would parade his literary ignorance, for my benefit, with a happy smile. On one occasion, when he spoke in a belittling way about Shakespeare, I was so incensed that I emptied a bowl of walnuts over his bald head. This merely produced a broadening of that wonderful smile as he contemplated his clever grandchild quite without rancour. He was a diabetic, and I can remember often peering into that comforting, loving face and noting that the whites of his eyes were a yellow colour. Then I would say chidingly,

"Grandpa, your sugar's up!" Of course it was. Sweetness was the keynote of his nature.

I didn't mean to use his picture as my object, in fact I had settled on something else. But, as I descended the stairs and passed it hanging there at the bottom – a sort of guardian of our household – and saw his little round belly, so indicative of a full, good life, and his concentration on his little hoard of money, I suddenly wanted to talk about him. The money was bagged up and then kept until delivery to the bank in his office swivel chair, where there was a deep hollow under the cushion where the chair sagged, and it just fitted snugly. Then he sat on it protectively for the duration, like one of his own hens. It was fun helping him count it too; money was so much more satisfyingly heavier and larger then. Piles of twelve pennies stood up stoutly and florins and half-crowns, and even the sixpences, had a body to them which equated to their value then. My aunt, his youngest daughter, still used to ride in to the bank on a horse sometimes with the money slung in saddle bags.

His son's widow, my aunt, who is incidentally Flick's mother, wants me to leave the picture to her son. Only son of his only son – and of course, I shall do so. But what will it mean to his children, who never met Grandpa? If they look at it carefully, something I hope.

D-DAY

Last Sunday was the 60th anniversary of D-day and I wore my father's medals, pinned on my jacket, all day. Not the big ones, just the little dress set – I didn't want to look ostentatious, but just quietly to commemorate his involvement in that momentous enterprise. There weren't any special medals – just the ordinary set that all soldiers have indicating where, when and how they have served. He was just an ordinary soldier and basically, I'm sure, a reluctant one as he was the most gentle and caring man. But he was quietly and firmly a patriot and a practical man who was a great believer in getting unpleasant jobs over and done with efficiently and with the minimum fuss.

I can't record any great stories about D-day or the subsequent liberation campaign because, like most non-professional soldiers of those times, he never talked about his experiences afterwards. He put it all behind him, as far as he could, but of course it left its legacy – in his case one of claustrophobia. We never talked about that either, although my mother and I knew about it and tried to ease his path. It wouldn't have been in keeping with his upbringing in a strict Methodist home, as one of four brothers who were all jolly good chaps, not to have been basically ashamed of such a weakness and while he accepted that these things happened, you didn't give in to them. But my parents changed to the early service where the congregation was sparse, he didn't go to the rugby matches when there was likely to be a crowd, and when I started working in the theatre and he could not bear not to see me, I always got him a seat at the end of the aisle where he could quietly get up and leave if necessary, and because he could he usually did not need to.

This was a result of being cooped up below in a stuffy transport ship for longer than had been expected owing to the bad weather, on rough seas, and with the thought of what was to come hanging over them all. Just an ordinary experience at that time for so many but one, I'm sure, no-one ever forgot. His particular transport struck a small mine or something similar which damaged that end of the boat. Miraculously there was no loss of life, though a number of motor bikes stored there were blown to bits. Not exactly nerve calming I'm sure. I don't remember which beach he landed on and I never heard what happened there but I know that on D-day plus two my mother had a telephone call from a BBC war correspondent. Again, I don't remember his name although my mother knew it – why don't we ever record these things? – but he had just returned to this country. He said to her,

"I slept last night on a beach, alongside your husband. He is **well** and sends his love and wants you to know there were no officer fatalities in his battalion." This was typical of my father's thought for others to send such a message. He knew that my mother was in touch with all the other wives as she had long been a camp-follower and knew most of them personally and so would instantly be on the telephone to them. The "officer" bit sounds very class-conscious but that's how the army was then and probably is still to some extent. It didn't mean that my father hadn't great compassion for the fate of all other ranks but he was a realist and the officers were the people you socialised with and therefore cared for individually. He was a captain and also, due to his no-nonsense organising skills, a very fine adjutant. He also got on well with all ranks because he was a very modest and unassuming man with little idea of his own worth. In fact, I don't think the concept ever occurred to him – he was always too busy thinking about other people.

I know no more about what happened in the ensuing months until Christmas time, when I know he was in Paris because he sent me Bernadette. A magnificent doll who arrived miraculously on Christmas Eve.

After the victory in Europe he was sent out east to Malaya where he picked up another legacy – a yearly recurrence of mild malaria which was rather like flu and with which he would retire to bed, yellow and shaking, for forty-eight hours, and then recover till the next year. Fortunately for him, if not for the Japanese, the atom bombs were dropped before they had to invade Japan.

My mother had been very apprehensive, naturally, when he sailed for the East and when we heard about the posting I had attempted to help her by writing a letter to the War Office, suggesting he not go as he was needed at home. The letter began.

"Honourable Sirs of the War Office", and there is one sentence I remember because my mother often quoted it later. This was it. "I am only nine years old, my grandfather who is looking after the business is ill and my mother has had little experience without my father"! Well, he could be thankful for that, anyway!

The letter was signed "Yours faithfully, Jill Martell – a soldier's daughter." That's what I was alright, and that's what I became again last Sunday – a soldier's daughter, and proud of it.

A TALE OF TWO DEMESNES

When returning from London on the train the other day and gazing out of the window, as one does when approaching the home station, I could not believe for a moment how much the landscape had changed since my youth. I grew up in Kempston when it was, and felt like, a village and not the overcrowded suburb of Bedford it seems today.

I was particularly lucky in the open spaces available to me. One set of grand-parents lived at Kempston Manor, with its spacious grounds running down to the river, where they actually included an island, reached in my early years by a fallen tree trunk with a taut rope handhold and later by a rustic bridge. My grandfather was very into the rustic after the war. Rustic benches abounded and were bestowed willy-nilly on members of the family and he even replaced our iron railings, removed for conversion to munitions in wartime, with yards of improbable `rustic' fencing.

The manor itself was an unremarkable building, whatever dwelling William the Conqueror's niece Judith (originally given the land by her illustrious Uncle) had erected being long gone, but the grounds were a delight. There were several `spinneys', heavy with the smell of box and the drowsy sound of wood pigeons, spacious lawns, the remains of a moat, some very old stables, an extensive fruit and vegetable garden. But best of all was the enchanted walled garden built of very old brick and trapping the sun so it seemed always filled with a warm scented haze emanating from the raspberries, loganberries, peaches and apricots espaliered inside its walls. Grandpa kept the key of this haven and we were only allowed in if he accompanied us, but this only elevated it to the status of `Secret Garden' - a book we all read in those days. Just outside our Nirvana was an old potting shed redolent of earth and onions and a small tadpole-filled pond with beside it, an ancient crab-apple tree. From the branches of this tree, the legend goes; a young lad bent on stealing the crab-apples, looked across at the window opposite and saw the Manor ghost - a gentleman in a periwig seated at a desk, busily writing. The boy was so startled that he fell out of the tree and broke his leg. This last, I know to be true as my grandfather showed me the newspaper clipping. I am not sure about the bewigged gentleman! The room he favoured with his occasional presence was solitary, off the wide landing halfway up the main staircase and I know my parents occupied this for a while after their marriage, without undue visitations.

My most vivid memories of childhood activities in these grounds were of playing croquet under the menacing branches of a truly enormous cedar tree with Great Aunt Ada, a headmistress and chapel-goer of great rectitude, who cheated regularly and blatantly, thought we never dared say so; of digging laborious trenches which we covered with branches, twigs and leaves in the hope of entrapping the gardener, our enemy; of escaping from an extra-long boring sermon from our grandfather in the Methodist chapel to follow a secret route home through the spinney and bounce out suddenly at sad Uncle Eric who was a little childish but most satisfyingly and vocally dismayed. Happy Days!

But at the Manor joy was never unconfined. Those Grandparents were rather formal and rigid and Grandma was fanatical about Sunday observance and good behaviour at all times. Grandpa, it is true, was very generous, liking to shower the whole family with gifts of whatever was his current obsession, from garish pink satin coronation handkerchiefs with the Queen's head embossed in gold, to cases of impossibly sweet sherry, grandfather clocks and of course, Rusticana. I can picture him now sitting at the head of his dinner table, cracking and peeling the famous Kempston walnuts to pass round and in between, beaming at us with his hands clasped on his full round stomach, while his thumbs rotated endlessly round one another.

But my maternal grandparents were farmers living at Springfield Dairies at the bottom of Spring Road on land leased from Dr Bowers, who kept a private asylum across the road for people whom in those unenlightened days, we did not hesitate to term 'loonies' but were probably nothing of the sort. In those days in our family we did not say 'round the bend' but 'over the road'. Here were more vast open spaces, presided over by Grandparents the antithesis of the others in their loving tolerance, shared with a network of Aunts, Uncles and cousins who liked nothing better than to get together on any occasion and excuse they could think of. One family lived further down Spring Road. Their domain bordered on College Street where my Uncle's family had a leather factory surrounded by several of their houses and boasting a sports field which connected at its upper end with my grandparents' farm. This we regarded as an extensive playground solely for our benefit and never mind the factory workers. And this field it was that I was contemplating from the train the other day, for the land is now entirely covered with houses, which completely obscure the view of my relatives' erstwhile homes. Indeed the same fate has overtaken the Manor grounds. Housing estates have been spawned on both sites and have effectively blotted out the past.

Once a year, on August Bank Holiday, the family took over pitch and pavilion alike for a daylong cricket match. There was no such thing as an eleven - anybody who wished to play went in to bat. The rules were simply that we started with the very youngest with a soft ball and a shorter pitch and worked our way upwards, the very youngest being allowed three chances before they were out. Fielding was sporadic, everybody was expected to do a stint but it need not be continuous. My Grandpa was the umpire, wearing his old brown farm overall and scrupulously changing a piece of cow cake from one pocket to the other to record the overs. He also cheerfully wore all the discarded pieces of clothing tossed in his direction and these were many and various considering my family's propensity for `dressing up'. Outfits were imaginative and appropriate or very much otherwise. One year an Uncle dressed as WG Grace, with full beard, but he wasn't a very competent bat, though a very safe pair of hands behind the wicket, particularly as the bowling was somewhat erratic. He later took over Umpire duties along with my Uncle who became renowned for breaking his leg in that role, though without holding up play for more than ten minutes while he was removed to hospital! In between stints at the wicket my Aunts produced miracles of sustaining and appetizing food in the pavilion. The sun, naturally, always shone brightly on us. Just as it was cold and frosty but never raining when we had our Guy Fawkes bonfire and fireworks in the same field. We wore fancy dress for that event too, even though it was dark. At the far end of the field the gate was always open to my grandparents' farm - yet another idyllic playground. We came in by the old stables with the two shire horses and the ponies that pulled the milk floats. At right angles were the pigsties and behind them Granny's kitchen garden, smaller than the one at the Manor and tended exclusively by herself, whence came the potatoes and peas and carrots whose taste lives in memory as unequalled now by supermarket fare. Then on past cowsheds and dairy and rick-yard with silos - great pits for jumping into when they were empty - threading your way through the marauding chickens, who had never heard of free-range, but were everywhere; their inquisitive beaks threatening my calves, vulnerable above inadequate ankle socks. Some of them thought they should live in the kitchen where Granny would chase them away as we got our fingers into her bowl of cake-mixture or the magic cupboard with a sliding door where resided the currants, raisins and sultanas. We would give her a hand to beat the Yorkshire pudding mixture which was belaboured for a very long time by all, then to be cooked under the meat so that it was succulent with juice in the middle and risen and crusty round the outside. No wonder we escaped so often through the field to the farm.

As I flash by the hideously boring housing estate in the train today, I seem to see myself and my cousins standing on the fence and waving to the driver and fireman on the lovely old steam trains, who would usually wave back - how we hated it when the early diesel engines came through. Hardly proper trains at all. I see our colourful costumes under the August sun, remember the naughty boys who would climb over the fence to lay pennies on the line for the trains to flatten and I hear the voice of my small cousin with the speech difficulties: `I'm doin' u' a barm a beel way'. This being translated means: `I am going to the farm the field way'.

How I wish, just once, I could do that very thing today.

SOUTHWOLD

My association with Southwold goes back a long way. You could say even to before I was born, as my parents used to holiday there. My own first memories are of wartime Southwold when my father was stationed in St Felix School, a high class girls' school whose pupils I was later to see walking in demure 'crocodiles', dressed in un-flattering, sage-green, severely cut jackets and skirts. The army much appreciated the comfortable billet and were very entertained by a notice in the dormitory reading 'Ring bell if you require a mistress in the night'! At this time my father's Bren-Gun Carriers (I thought of them as his) were snugly parked, draped in camouflage nets, under a row of trees which border the school grounds and the road. This sort of image colours my early impressions of Southwold, as did the barbed wire on the beach, and the severely truncated pier which gave the impression of having been drawn in, like an ancient drawbridge, to prevent invaders from nearby Holland across the water from popping in to disturb the local Dad's Army. And, no, I wasn't actually part of this, or the regular army at the time, but my mother and I had become camp followers consequent upon the fact of doctors having recommended that I take time off school and 'get some sea air' because of a sequence of childhood illnesses from which I had recently suffered, and also upon the fact of my mother's natural desire to see as much of my father as she could while she was able. We got our fill of sea air around the country and it took some time to persuade me, after the war, that barbed wire wasn't as natural a feature of the seaside as buckets and spades.

After the war my next encounter with Southwold was on a month long holiday when my family, together with an aunt and uncle and various cousins, took a bungalow there. I fell in love with the place all over again. The beach is not an ideal one for children, being of uncompromising shingle, and there is a current in the sea which means you usually get swept sideways and do not come out opposite your clothes. There is a long row of beach huts standing on a raised promenade. It can often be a long jump down to the shingle, depending how the latest tide has left the stones, and the distance from hut to sea can be hard on the feet. But the huts are painted in differing bright colours and they are roomy, with space to change at the back, room to picnic at a table inside, fresh water on tap behind the huts and ample opportunity for heating this on various devices as sophisticated, or not, as you wish. The double doors, when opened, fold back to the sides of a veranda where you can sit and contemplate the sea, sheltered on either side from the wind, which is often very strong on the East Coast.

At one end of the beach, which does have some sand down at the shoreline, is a sandier part, still sprinkled with pebbles, with what we always called 'the dunes' at the top end; hilly mounds of sand with large clumps of coarse grass sprouting from them and, in season, many bright yellow lupins. The dunes continue until cut off by the river which bounds Southwold on one side and separate it from the artists' colony at Walberswick on the other side. The mouth of this river is extremely dangerous and has been the scene of one or two tragic accidents to holiday makers, boating and ignoring warnings from local fisherman.

At the other end of the beach is the aforementioned pier, now splendidly restored and elongated, but then just as short and stubby. At the shore end of the pier there was a refreshment room (Later a pub, The Neptune) and an amusement room – I can't dignify it with the name of arcade – with various penny-in-the-slot machines, solidly built and massive, which would sell for a fortune at antique fairs today. One of these, an old favourite with the cow jumping over the moon while the dish eloped surreptitiously with the spoon and the cat fiddled the while, was still there many years later when my son was very young and, though we went decimal the year he was born, pennies were still made available somehow. The machine had gone by the time his sister arrived but had obviously made a great impression on him as, having been told she was in my tummy, he put his eye to my navel and remarked,

"I can't see it, the baby! I'll put a penny in!" Nowadays, alas, the machines are electronically and digitally sophisticated and a great deal of killing and blowing up is involved. Oh, for those innocent times! The only other diversion at the time of our après-war holiday in Southwold, was a merry-go-round outside the amusement room and a little putting green opposite. Later, in my children's day, there was a boating lake beside it and the pub had arrived, where boys on motor bikes congregated on Saturday night.

Southwold is a pretty place with a great variety of architecture in its houses and cottages, many of which are grouped around 'Greens', (South Green, St James' Green etc). This is a consequence of a bad fire, or it may have been two separate fires, in the distant past when whole chunks of the town were wiped out and in re-building they left these attractive greens. Another very distinctive feature of Southwold in those days was the number of different ships' figure heads which were attached to the walls of various houses, leaning out and leering from high up as if to try and get a glimpse of the sea. These too are long gone, victims of the current craze for 'antiques and collectibles', but I hope at least a source of profit to the inhabitants. And then there were the guns at Gun Hill, a raised hill at the end of the central , large South Green; six of them pointing out to sea alongside the coastguard's little observatory, all of them relics of the battle of Sole Bay, Southwold's great claim to fame. A sea battle against the Dutch which was commemorated 300 years later in nineteen seventy something (six, I think) when all the shopkeepers and publicans and many of their customers dressed in period costume to go about their business for a week, and Adnam's, the local brewery which fills the town with the scent of hops to compete with the sea breezes, produced their celebrated new brew, 'Broadside'.

As children, after the war, we were content to play on the beach, French cricket and such innocent amusements, and to roam on the common - which stretches on one side of Southwold down to the river - and around the 'Harbour', which is a few hundreds of yards up-river from the sea and boasts a fine array of fishing craft and now, increasingly, leisure craft. Here is situated the wonderful, old 'Harbour Inn', with a plaque high up on the wall at the second storey to mark the water level in the big floods in the fifties. At the time of our early holiday there was also a boat just above the harbour where a ferryman would row you across to Walberswick to have tea in a little cottage garden, always full of wasps in my memory, and to visit the exhibition of local artists' pictures. The light around Walberswick and indeed Southwold has a wonderful clear quality, much appreciated by artists, and sometimes I have looked along the beach at Southwold towards the town and seen all the buildings as if they had a sharp line drawn around them. The outstanding feature being of course, the lighthouse, which stands back from the shore in a street in the town and relays its messages out to sea. At that time it was not open to the public though these days, in response to Southwold's growing popularity with visitors, you can climb up to the top. But we used to love watching it illuminating the sea with its four flashes separated by an interval which was much disputed between us cousins as it depended on how fast you counted. I think I got to about fourteen or fifteen. I have never timed it since, preferring to leave it a bit of mystery and enchantment. So I don't climb it either.

We had one exciting adventure when roaming the common in Famous Five style. We came upon something metal in one of the dykes which cross the common, which we were convinced was an un-exploded bomb. We had tremendous fun speculating and dashing home to tell our parents. I believe in fact it was a shell, or part of one but, alas, already well and truly exploded. It was a happy month when the sun always shone and the garden of our bungalow, also boasting a memento from the Germans in the shape of a deep pit where something unpleasant had fallen, nevertheless managed to hold our interest with the fruits of numerous red, white and black currant bushes.

In the early sixties my parents bought a holiday home in Southwold which we were to enjoy for the next twenty-one years, along with a bright blue painted beach hut called Jo-Jo, after the eldest daughter of the vendors. Our house was not a pretty little cottage (those tended to be more expensive) but a three story house with five bedrooms and a basement flat, then inhabited by Mrs Swan, a splendid Goanese widow of an Irishman, who had somehow ended up in this remote spot. We took her on with the house and for some years, until she died of a totally neglected cancer, which she never mentioned to anyone, we enjoyed her warmth and love of children and her rabidly British, Tory, attitude to politics and the life around her. She didn't hold with foreigners and her strictures on members of the government were both harsh and entertaining. But whenever we arrived there we would find little presents awaiting us and our dog never failed to find a squeaky toy awaiting his eager shaking and eventual demolition.

We needed a large house as I have a very large family of aunts, uncles and cousins, all of whom enthusiastically enjoyed their holidays there. One or two got engaged there – it was that kind of place – and several used it for their honeymoons. My parents and I enjoyed it equally in the winter, when the town was free of visitors or day trippers and we could enjoy the company of the many local people we got to know, notably Mrs Jarvis, wife of the coastguard, who lived next door and who was the successor to Mrs Swan in keeping an eye – and a duster – on the house when we were not there and welcoming us when we arrived with thoughtful preparations and the latest local news. She was an amazing woman – thin as a rake – and I don't think she ever sat down. Quite apart from keeping her house spotless – and often ours as well – she would pop up in the most unlikely places, explaining she was just giving a hand while so-and-so was in hospital, visiting a relative, popping into Lowestoft or just having a lie-down. The whole town seemed to call on her to keep their businesses running and no local event took place without her involvement.

These events were many in Southwold. It was a town which liked tradition and celebrating. Adnams were hard put to it to find new names for the special brews they always produced for the great occasions. But the traditional events were also pursued with the same energy and enthusiasm. Christmas in Southwold was an enchantment with almost every shop, very unusually in those early days of the sixties, before the advent of abundant cheap shiny glass and excessive electrical effects, having a Christmas tree outside down the long line of the main street. It was tasteful and it was magical. Easter and Whitsun brought more outdoor events. The fair on South Green on Trinity Sunday was none of your tired old village fetes. It was illuminated by the local, whole hearted enjoyment of an occasion. The pram race round Southwold's many pubs by members of the local football team, with one member dressed as a baby in the pram and the other in skirt and bonnet pushing it, was hilarious. At each pub they paused to drink a pint each with much jocularity and encouragement from the bystanders and they often ended up with the 'baby; pushing the pram and the 'mother' having a well earned rest inside.

And then there were the Morris-men. No source of slightly superior mirth, these. They were well respected and always welcomed and enlivened all occasions with their dedicated dancing. But they were great fellows with a sense of humour and fun, no bespectacled earnestness but a professionalism that made them always admired. My daughter, when she was young, adored them, and made my mother buy her tiny bells to tie on her ankles while she leaped about the shore waving all available handkerchiefs.

My husband, meanwhile, was becoming an accepted member of the fishing fraternity. He did not go out long-lining from the harbour although we were very happy to sample their catch, but he became very friendly with a local lad, who later took over the very flourishing fishing=tackle shop, and who was dedicated to beach casting. He would spend hours practising this art from the shore and taught my husband a great deal, especially how to avoid getting the dreaded 'bird's nest' of tangled line by judicious management of the complicated reel. He used to go in for competitions locally and was a frequent winner but my husband contented himself with putting his knowledge to the test on shore and at the end of the pier catching us a respectable amount of cod and whiting to consume, including the big one which didn't get away, which I have described elsewhere.

Southwold's railway was closed down in the thirties and the track has disappeared, although you can still see where it arrived across the end of the common. I'm not sure how it managed this across the creek which bounds Southwold on the inshore side and is responsible for the fact that it has stayed compact without any straggling growth. Thus you enter Southwold across a little bridge, Might's Bridge over Buss creek. My husband and I would often arrive at the railway station at nearby Halesworth and immerse ourselves in the Suffolk atmosphere at the little pub nearby until we were either fetched by car from Southwold by my father or, if he were not there we would catch a bus. When we all arrived together by car our first port of call on the Friday evening was to the Red

Lion, where the landlord obtained magnificent tasty steaks from an acquaintance who supplied the meat for the liners out of Lowestoft or Yarmouth. This was served on a block of wood rather than a plate along with succulent chips and, as it was washed down with plentiful red wine, became known as Steak on the Plonk, rather than the Landlord's designation of Steak on the Plank. And thus would a weekend of delight begin. Southwold however boasts a pub for all occasions and our other favourites were the Lord Nelson, on the edge of the cliff above the sea, low ceilinged and beamed with snug corners and inviting dart bard, and the Sole Bay, under the shadow of the lighthouse,, kept by our dear friends Vic and Marge with whom we passed many happy evenings swapping stories and munching the fresh shrimps invariably brought in by one of the many fishermen who made it their local And, of course, the Harbour Inn, vast but welcoming where visitors sit side by side with fishermen and there is a really excellent standard of music and song in the evenings. These were our favourites but we weren't proud – we patronised them all – not forgetting the small but popular fish and chip shop whose wares were truly fit for the Gods.

Nowadays Southwold has become almost trendy. It certainly boasts some very up-market shops and a couple of the minor pubs and some of the shops have been turned into restaurants to cater for the growing crowds. The season is longer and the bed-and-breakfasts are more plentiful but the buildings are still there and beautiful, even though I may mourn the passing of some of the old businesses. Like the baker's shop which provided such fresh bread everyday and at Easter the wonderful hot-cross buns, thoughtfully ordered for us by Mrs Jarvis. Denny's the wonderful old fashioned, high-class tailors and haberdashers with its ancient dark interior and discreet clothing display; the old-time grocer's, Mr Bumstead, where we would order provisions for the week and have them sent round; the hardware shop reminiscent of the two Ronnie's Fork Handles sketch, where you could buy one nail if you needed it; the tiny crowded toy shop across from our house which stocked buckets and spades, windmills and ice-cream and could produce from odd corners exciting metal wind-up toys which hadn't been seen elsewhere since before the war. All these I remember nostalgically, but life has moved and Southwold with it. Many of our fishermen friends are dead now, but the spirit is still there in the town. There are enough natives who think in the same old way and bring their own fresh outlook to the blending of old tradition with modern life. Southwold adapts – and embraces.

The beautiful East Anglian flint-walled church, St Edmunds, stands proudly on its Green, light and airy, smelling now of salt air, now of hops and presided over by the medieval figure of Southwold Jack, high on the wall inside striking a bell with his hammer as he did when I entered the church as a bride in 1969. And I hope he will do the same this September when, after a letter to the Archbishop of Canterbury conveying, I hope, some of the feelings we have for this place, and the payment of £130 my daughter, no longer a resident, but possessing a special licence and a great love in her heart, is married there, as I was.

THANK YOU CARLOTTA!

I knew, of course, that I was destined to be a writer.

Hadn't I written my first novel when I was six years old and ten months; an opus with numbered pages, for goodness sake, and a list of contents? The affecting climax when the little heroine's father came home from the war and, with her mother, the three of them sat before a blazing fire (my father was a coal merchant) toasting crumpets for tea, still makes me weep. I don't know where the butter came from in those days of austerity and crumpets are simply hopeless without lashings of butter. And had I not written a wide variety of poems such as "Ode to a German Measle" (the war still affecting me there) and my mother's two favourites, "Moonlight Revels", a simperingly pretty piece about fairies which did however contain the interesting couplet *"On every side came stealing the merry pipes of Pan,-Behind a bush concealing he's only half a man "*!!!

The other, which I still have an affection for, was entitled "Shopping", and consisted of an enquiry in several of the main shops in Bedford for an item they patently did not sell, complete with their somewhat zany replies.

   e.g. *I went to the Cadena,*

      "Have you a Vacuum Cleaner?"

      They said in a fluster

      We've only one duster".

Or my mother's favourite:

      I went into Boots

      I said "any suits"?

      They said "No, no clothes,

And then swore dreadful oaths!"

Well, of course, I was an extremely talented writer indeed!

All this was to change when I was nine years old and wrote my first play "Carlotta ", written especially for my cousin and best friend who was mad about horses. Nothing daunted, I included as a climax to this stirring drama a three-heat horse race to take place on stage. And my family, being great lovers of "dressing up" and all natural performers, actually put it on.

It was war-time and so we had a distinct lack of male members of the family to take part and so my mother donned a tweed suit and bowler hat as the heroine's father; one of my aunts in corduroys and boots was Farmer Brown; her husband, the only male, was splendidly bow-legged and straw chewing as Mr Heathcliff, the groom, and my mother's youngest sister starring as the villain, Mr Macclesfield, was resplendent in top hat and tails with the largest most villainous black moustache you ever saw. My uncle, the groom, doubled as curtain puller, lighting man and sound effects, horses' hooves a speciality. Not coconut shells, it being war-time, but subtle and effective use of a small drum.

The plot centred on the efforts of the villainous Mr Macclesfield to gain possession of the heroine, Carlotta's horse, which she kept in a field owned by the friendly Farmer Brown and which was tended by the eccentric groom, Heathcliff. In some mysterious way, the ownership of the horse would all be resolved by the result of the aforementioned three-heat horse race. This was very tense and exciting. Carlotta nobly won the first heat. In the second the villain villainously won by means of a foul - my aunt's finest moment, this. Or perhaps it was eclipsed by her realistic death agonies in the third heat when she fell off her horse and proceeded to expire after somewhat surprisingly bequeathing her own horse to Carlotta with her final gasp. The actual line was remarkably un-PC even for those days and ran "Black Jew! Black Jew! I don't want her, give her to Carlotta! "

For myself, I wrote the modest role of the heroine's sister, Sylvia, whose principal function was loyally to encourage and cheer Carlotta at every turn and to assist in grooming the horse! I can still vividly remember the first proper rehearsal which took place out of doors in the field behind my aunt's house, because it was a beautiful sunny day. I threw myself with enthusiasm into my role which, of course, I already knew by heart, and felt a warm exhilaration running through me. The sun had never been so bright, nor the grass so green, and I had never loved my family so passionately. I heard my aunt saying to my mother, "Gill is amazing - she can really act." And I knew this was true and that an actor was what I was going to be and what I had always been, and that there was an immense and exciting power in me. It was a feeling I was to know again and again and which made up for all the times when life and work weren't so good and when one asks oneself "Why am I doing this?" I knew why on that sunny afternoon and I know it still. It isn't a self-glorifying power - the 'question of one's ego is quite different and separate. This one is more like being in touch with all humanity, and even all nature and just for a while being a sort of effortless channel for it. Perhaps for this reason I was quite content with my subservient role as heroine's loyal sister and gave it all I'd got. But perhaps my actor's ego was born when I wrote myself an epilogue to speak. To deliver this, I hastily undid my tight, unflattering plaits and let my hair ripple over my shoulders, glamorous beyond words in my own imagination, and modestly clutching a bouquet of flowers I had insisted be presented me in my character as author.

But I was a writer no longer ...

I was all actor.

TEDDY BOYS

My aunt had a weakness for giving meals and a temporary roof-over-the-head to young out of work actors whom she seemed to encounter quite easily, particularly since I suspect the first one set a word-of-mouth system going in London.

"If you're broke and you fancy ruralising in a nice informal household with some very good cooking – just for a week or so ...." The first of these was the young Laurence Harvey, who came down quite a few times before dropping us abruptly when he got his 'big break', and whom I chiefly remember for the nerve-racking speed with which he drove my aunt's car.

But by far our longest association was with an Australian actor called Laon Maybanke, though I doubt this was the name he was born with. He may have come from the Antipodes but his accents were pure, refined camp, in the style of Noel Coward. He was gay, of course, but this was something only dimly apprehended by us young teenagers, and never, in those days, discussed. He had jet-black hair and a tanned complexion with strong features, particularly the nose. He moved with languid, balletic grace and had a very good figure. Inevitably his very intermittent and obscure acting career mutated – I won't say degenerated – into one of minor modelling jobs. I can clearly remember the day, though not the identity of the magazine, but it was thick and glossy, when he proudly displayed to us a whole series of photographs of himself in smart, but still slightly camp, Edwardian costume which he said was about to become the latest fashion. We duly admired the pictures, and indeed thought him very handsome, but did not believe for a moment that this somewhat effete-looking style would ever catch on. And indeed there was quite a gap between the up-market black and white suits and shirts which he displayed and the 'Teddy-Boy' image taken up so enthusiastically by quite a different class of person with its bright colours, shoelace ties and pointed boots. But the provenance was undoubtedly there and you heard it first from us!

Dear Laon! He became quite a part of the family for some years and when we started giving 'concerts' on a regular basis — an enterprise I shall describe elsewhere — he constituted himself our producer and did indeed help us elevate our amateur standards into a certain professionalism. I myself learned quite a lot from him, particularly in the matter of comedy timing, a skill which has to be basically intuitive, but which can be honed by imitation of a good example, which he certainly was. His party piece, I recall, was a rendition of the story of 'Goldilocks and the three bears', in a pseudo-Germanic accent in which the jokes were appropriately Edwardian-risqué. Some of them were nevertheless above our innocent, young, early fifties heads, but I recognised and appreciated his basic sense of style. He should have been an Edwardian I feel — he even taught me how to open and close a fan with panache. What attracted the later Teddy-Boys to the style he had so proudly exhibited to us in that magazine I am not sure. I suppose it was a reaction to the drab economies of our wartime costumes; and the characters who had been the wide boys of the war-time black market — the 'Walkers' of Dad's Army, found in this exaggerated form of Edwardian costume an expression of their cheeky, furtive but unrepentant souls. Even Laon's abundant black hair longer at the back than was normal in those times, as befitted an 'actor' and brushed into a wave at the front, was a forerunner of the Teddy-Boy 'duck's arse' style. But he presented a picture of elegance and would have been horrified to be described as a 'thug'.

He dropped out of our lives and I met him only a couple of decades later when I found he was working as an extra on a TV show I was doing. We had a meal together in the canteen and I found him remarkably unchanged. Grey hair had only added to his distinguished appearance, his figure was as elegant as ever and he was augmenting his earnings by dabbling in antiques, particularly grandfather clocks, which he bought, repaired and sold. He must have been a great anachronism in the Australia of his early days which worshipped only rugged masculinity and it is not surprising he escaped to England, and there took refuge in our more elegant past. Laon Maybanke — first of the Teddy-Boys — last of the Edwardians!

OUR "CONCERTS"

My Mother's family were always up for performing at any time and in any situation. My Father's family were not at all the same, except that I suspect there was a strong streak of drama being suppressed in my grandmother with her strict Baptist upbringing and her close association with the Bible. But, oddly, only second to the Bible did she revere Dickens and all his works. I suppose she thought them moral, but personally I think it was the drama in Dickens which secretly appealed. She also had a poem which she occasionally recited entitled "Edinburgh after Flodden", and which was distinctly O.T.T. in her rendition. I can still hear her now declaiming in sepulchral tones "News of Battle / Who hath brought it!" My grandfather in his Methodist pulpit got pretty dramatic at times too, but was so long winded it nullified the effect. I thought his gestures could have done with some working on too!

But in my Mother's family we were all for comedy with plenty of lively music thrown in. This Granny and Grandpa used to sing duets from things like "Flora Dora" and, one I loved, "The Belle of New York". There was a big dressing up box in the cupboard at the farm, full of a most eclectic supply of garments and decorations and this could be raided at any time. My Mother and her three sisters and one brother were always devising entertainments for anybody passing through who could be persuaded to sit down a minute and watch. My Mother, as the eldest and also the literary one, wrote most of the dialogue and was much addicted herself to dressing up as a queen (preferably a Fairy Queen). Thus garbed she would rather meanly sit on a chair perched on top of the table and direct her siblings to do the tidying up. This habit of hers was deeply resented and to this day, in my Aunt Joan's family and those of her children and grandchildren, the person who sits comfortably while others are doing the washing up, or whatever, is described as 'doing a Molly' – my Mother's name.

My Aunt Joan was very talented in dancing, particularly the ballet, and would have made it her career had she not decided at an early age to marry my Uncle Frank, who had very little to say in the matter. She remained a most graceful mover and of very neat and elegant appearance all her life and her great party piece was to do the splits. But in order to make a proper performance of it she would have to be persuaded and then there were many false starts and exaggerated warming-up before she obliged and sank down with great ease and much flourish. Her alternative performance was just the same. She made a great feature of the reluctance and the run up to her 'dance', and would finally do two or three steps singing "Ta-ra-ra-Boom-de-ay" and then subside amid much applause and refuse to do any more. Only a year before she died, at 85, she had watched her Canadian grand-daughter dancing and after applauding said "can you do this?", and proceeded to pick up her foot and hold it over her head. She it was who encouraged and supported all my generation in their performing careers. Both her daughters did ballet and the second one, Vicki, who now lives in Canada, has two children in the ballet world there and a daughter who plays the harp. Auntie Joan's son, Charles, was a very quiet boy much subdued by his lively and talented sisters, but in his teens he suddenly began, most painfully to all of us and himself, to learn the violin. He became doggedly proficient and then his whole personality underwent a complete change. He was suddenly voluble and loud and very funny and took his fiddle everywhere. He is married now to a lively lady who plays the accordion and the spoons and they do Morris Dancing and play together at all the weddings for miles around. I also owe a great debt to his mother. My own was rather inclined to understand and shield my basic shyness and lack of confidence. My Aunt Joan would have none of it and pushed me firmly in the direction she knew I longed and ought to go.

As to my Mother's other siblings, her youngest sister, Paul and her brother Clifford (who was Flick's father) had enormous comic talent. Both of them had an innate sense of comic timing, which cannot be taught and only with difficulty learned. Paul it was who played the villain in my celebrated play, Carlotta, of which I have written and very splendid she was too. Clifford's forte was mime and he and Paul and his wife, Heather, devised a series of 'scenes' in which the principal ingredient was mime. Heather is very good at garrulous old ladies and any talking was done by her, but it was Clifford's reactions and facial expression that made the scene. At all of our frequent family parties someone was bound to say "Do the bus scene". This was everybody's favourite and involved all of them squeezing past each other and strap hanging on a bus. Throughout the scene you were constantly aware of them swaying to the motions of the bus in perfect unison so that the illusion was complete. I can't remember what the scene was all about – they usually had very effective and simple themes – but I can remember Clifford having a newspaper and the other two attempting to read over his shoulder, and the old gag of him folding it smaller and smaller until he ended up on all fours trying to shield it from them. In another "scene" I seem to remember he wore a large black fake moustache on his lugubrious face and ended up getting a cream bun squashed all over it. Simple stuff but we all laughed until we cried.

So, with this kind of provenance it was not surprising that some of my cousins and a few friends ended up forming a sort of concert party, though we didn't have a pier to perform on the end of, and that these entertainments became more and more large scale and professional over the course of six to eight years. They started in a small way soon after Joan, Frank, my cousin Sue et al had moved into her deceased grandparents' house. They didn't have far to go as their own house had been built, a perfect little thirties gem just ripe for an episode of Poirot, in the grounds of the Sanders senior home. These contained, among other things, a vast garage which would have accommodated a couple of large vehicles in days gone by. Here we erected our first stage – not a platform affair but with proper curtains and a door to a largish room off the garage which served as a dressing room and entrance for the actors. The main door admitted the audience to the other half of the garage. We had a lot of family and a great many friends so the house was packed for a couple of performances. I remember my Aunt Paul perched up at the back on a window sill with George, the brother of her dead fiancé who she had lost at Dunkirk, and both of them whistling and barracking a little as well as leading the applause.

We had a better mannered audience later when, by popular request, we transferred what had become an annual Christmas show to the larger premises provided by Uncle Frank, who had had to move the hides stored in a deconsecrated chapel used by his leather factory. The hides had left behind a rather strong smell but we had a vastly superior space in which to work. Another cousin, living in Spring Road, who had a job making hats for Aage Thaarup, hat makers to royalty, and who was consequently very artistic, painted interesting designs on some Hessian curtains which could be controlled from the wings, and long-suffering Uncle Frank fixed us up some proper lighting, complete with dimmers.

Enter Laon Maybanke, whom I have described elsewhere, my aunt's pet, out-of-work actor, model and frequent guest. He took over the direction of the shows from her and proceeded to give them a professional stamp. The format was that the first half comprised company songs and sketches interspersed with their latest dance numbers from Sue and Vicki, and almost always, a dramatic monologue from me and one comedy monologue. Sue and I also did duologues, among them Cecily and Gwendolyn and Rosalind and Celia. I was not fussy about appearing as a male or a female and cheerfully did some of Bernard Miles monologues alongside those of Joyce Grenfell and Beryl Reid in her character of 'Marlene from the Midlands'. Sue and I had our greatest success with a sketch of Cyril Fletcher and Betty Astell's called 'The Football Match', in which I as Cyril initiated my wife into the joys of early football hooliganism, in support of 'the 'Ammers', or West Ham United. The comedy came from the contrast between my measured tones in explaining the game to my meek little wife and my sudden mad dashes up and down the pitch urging them to slaughter the other team. This finishes with her deciding to support the other side and emulating my performance, squeaking her own mild defiance. Yes, well ….. You had to have been there.

Besides this display of our enormous talents we would do various quick-fire sketches brought back to us faithfully by Cousin Gerald, whose parents took him to Gorleston-on-Sea every summer and from whence he plundered the concert parties of Yarmouth for new material.

My mother had considerable talent as a lyric writer and would take various suitable popular songs and tailor the lyrics to our abilities and concerns. My cousin Vicki, five years younger than Sue and me always had a popular spot where she sang a song of my mother's devising with enormous and inappropriate confidence and, for a couple of years at least, very few front teeth. She had her own sense of timing – the pianist had to follow her – and she would forget lines and take prompts with a wide smile and even start again from the beginning if she felt like it.

I didn't mind doing my comic monologues but always felt that my dramatic pieces were out of place in this entertainment. I had to do Juliet taking her poison and Henrietta from the Barretts of Wimpole Street being tyrannised by her father – all this solo with imaginary people I might be addressing. It was no good – this was what everybody wanted and expected of me – they liked a good cry now and then.

The second half was taken up with a one act play of some kind – our best one was called "The Princess who never smiled", I recall - and was rounded off with a final rousing company song. Believe it or not this curious entertainment was extremely popular with various organisations in the town and we had to perform for the Mothers Union, Toc H, The League of Pity and various similar bodies. They all said they preferred it to a pantomime at Christmas. Those were naïve days.

As we were a concert party we had to have a compère to introduce the items and provide links whilst Joan was helping us change back stage and Laon, the director, insisted on my mother doing it. She was quite a shy person and was always horrified at the idea but Laon would see that she had a couple of gins before the show and would push her on so that she immediately got into a muddle and would correct herself and say," oh no, I meant to say this" or "I wasn't supposed to say that" and with gradually increasing assurance take the audience into her confidence and start lengthy explanations which she would suddenly cut short in dismay saying, "I can't really do this you know. I don't know why they make me. I shan't do it next year."

The audience loved her and Laon became quite hysterical in the wings egging her on with shouts of encouragement when she didn't seem to know how to get off the stage.

I am aware that this doesn't sound very professional at all and Laon was actually very strict with the rest of us. It's just that he knew that acts like Vicki and my mother should be left to connect with the audience, each in her own way – the one through over confidence and the other through a basic lack of it. There was an underlying awareness of how to handle an audience in all of my family – they never overstepped the mark. We ended up doing eight performances for 50 to 60 people in the latter years and it was an integral part of our Christmas.

Shows like ours, relying on basic naivety and charm with a little talent thrown in and a lot of energy and commitment would be laughed at today. Television has given us a spurious sophistication and slickness and is voracious in eating up new material. Families do not get together to make their own entertainment as we were lucky enough to do. Children are left to their solitary play stations and adults resort to their video tapes. The subtle joys of communication with a small audience are thus for the most part lost to them, and I do not think the mass hysteria of a Glyndebourne crowd or a Live Aid concert quite makes up for this profound loss.

CHURCHILL

I have only very vague and random memories of the day I accompanied my uncle to No. 10 Downing Street, where he was to present a large cheque to Sir Winston Churchill on his eightieth birthday. This money had been amassed through my uncle's newspaper as a thank you tribute, and the donations had ranged from substantial ones from firms to half-crowns from humble and grateful admirers. We were met at the door by a second cousin-several-times-removed who was on the staff at No. 10 at the time and who introduced me to Lady Clementine Churchill. She immediately said,

"Come and see his cakes!" We toured a room chock-full of birthday cakes, large and small, plain and fantastic, which had been sent him by a still grateful populace. I remember being impressed by one with a large icing-sugar rocket on it, pointing to the stars. I thought this very avant-garde and futuristic. Then we were in a room of little gilt and red plush chairs, drinking tea and eating what my sense of fitness, not my memory, tells me were cucumber sandwiches. The presentation was made, with speeches, and I took the somewhat flaccid hand of the Prime Minister in mine and shook it reverently, forswearing future washing. He seemed only interested in chatting to his two grandchildren, young Nicholas and Emma Soames whom he took alternately on his knee. Then I think he went to sleep! And we must have gone home.

MAKING AN ENTRANCE

I didn't intend to make my entrance into the professional stage such a dramatic one – well, such a comic one – well, both really.

I had been lucky enough to be asked to do a television performance of Chekhov's "The Proposal" with Richard Briars and Miles Malleson, in the holidays before my last term at RADA, resulting from the "Public Show" in which the Academy's work used to be show-cased before an audience comprising many fellow artistes, a lot of agents, producers from repertory companies etc. And before the TV show I had already got my provisional Equity Card – you had to do forty more weeks before you became a full member. I had also acquired an agent after the public show and had caught the eye of Robert Digby who ran the repertory company at Colchester and had offered me a season there – not even as an A.S.M. but as a juvenile character actress.

So there I was, sorted you would think. I can't remember the actual title of the first play I was in there, though I remember the play itself – a light comedy in which the leading actress, who is still one of my greatest friends and still working – unlike me, was having a much deserved success. My part as her secretary was smallish and easy to cope with, not a lot to do but a lot of popping in and out. I was not very popular when, in one of these entrances, I had some difficulty with the door sticking. I managed to enter alright, but with the door-knob still in my hand! A day later I inadvertently swept one of the vases on the mantelpiece to the floor, where it disobligingly came apart – probably already cracked I should think – good props were difficult to come by. However, in my character of secretary I was able to clear it up and dispose of it satisfactorily and I felt I had done quite well. I was not quite so happy the next day and nor was the electrician when, short sighted as I was, and no contact lenses in those days, I stumbled in the wings and fused two lamp brackets on stage.

Then came the Saturday Matinee. The leading lady had just swept off to her usual sure-fire gale of laughter developing into an exit round and I was waiting in the wings for the applause to hit the right level – beginning to die but not dead – and the moment was right for me to trip down the three steps for my entrance onto the empty stage. And that's exactly what I did – Trip! And fall headlong to concerned gasps from out front. Backstage they were also concerned, but not in a kindly way. I rose in great pain and, smiling bravely, limped through my mercifully short appearance and got myself off in good order into the wings.

Later, the leading man asked to see me in his dressing room and I went in some trepidation. But he was a kind man and he merely said,

"The company have asked me to remind you that you haven't joined a circus!"

I may say that the next week's play was "Claudia" in which I was given the juvenile lead, a part in which I was scarcely ever off stage. And I was obliged to play it, humiliatingly, with one red shoe on and one yellow bedroom slipper covering a multitude of crepe bandages. Rise above that, Gillian.

DOUBLE ACT

I was doing a school's tour based in Nottingham and, with others of the company, was in digs with Bill and Lucy Fisher. They were a splendid example of northern domesticity. (Alright, so Nottingham is midlands, but the great divide probably does begin, if not north of Watford as tradition has it, certainly between us and Leicester.) Bill and Lucy were the funniest double-act I had yet encountered in my new professional life. Lucy was a big woman, always to be seen in the conventional flowered overall, never off her feet, presiding over her kitchen with the door to the little parlour, where we ate and sat in the evenings, ever open, so that she could maintain a flow of conversation. This, in her case, consisted of flat, not-to-be-contradicted statements and comments on her husband's contributions which, although delivered in as soft a voice as hers was strident, she never missed. I think she felt she had to keep a watchful eye on him with us four young girls, and if not an eye then an eagle ear.

Bill certainly felt that his mission was to entertain us. In contrast to Lucy he was a small man who sat by the fire in his special chair and, as she never sat down, he never got up. Even when his meal was ready he simple propelled himself over to the table still sitting in the chair – which was not on wheels by any means – and after the meal he scrabbled his way back to the fire. He had a cough, acquired when he was down the pit, and a stammer probably acquired through trying to compete with Lucy's dictatorial conversational manner. I will never forget the "funny story" he tried to tell us on our first evening there – an old and well-tried chestnut.

"There was this w-woman got m-married, you see, and her mother said to her 'I'll tell you how to go on. When you're wed, k-keep a bit of something on in b-bed.' And a w-week later her husband says to her, 'is there any in-s-sanity in your family?' So she says, 'N-no, why?', and he says, 'well, you've b-been c-coming to bed all week with yer 'at on!" We laughed politely. Silence from the kitchen, then Lucy, who had no sense of humour, shouted, "Well Bill, maybe she wore a wig"!

Towards the end of our stay Bill astonished us all by proving he could not only stand on his legs but could go out. He selected me for a conducted tour of Nottingham by night. Lucy did not demur. By this time she saw me as no threat. I was not one of the pretty ones. He donned a very new-looking camel-haired coat – I don't suppose it got much wear – and an old cloth cap to emphasis his northern-ness and we sallied forth.

He took me first to the banks of the River Trent where, in the gloaming of the winter evening, he explained to me how pretty it looked in the spring with all the daffodils out. Nest we went to the Astoria ballroom and he took me round the side of some closed double doors through which music could be faintly heard. He made me put my ear to the crack, while he described the bright and lively scene within, with the coloured lights and frothy frocks. And finally he took me into the pub which he told me complacently I must never attempt to enter without the protection of so stalwart a champion as he. He shuffled up to the bar and said firmly: "Two rum-hots please." And rum-hots we drank. I expect I was grateful after our somewhat chilly tour!

Dear Bill and Lucy – I wonder what happened to them? When I was next in Nottingham that part of the town had been razed to the ground to make way for more modern developments. I wonder if the removal van carried them away with Bill still sitting in his chair, and Lucy standing behind him firmly shouting directions.

WEEKLY REP - FORTNIGHTLY

I feel very sorry for all those drama students attempting to find jobs in the business today. They work so much harder than we did and are so much more accomplished and competitive. They can all sing and dance, as well as act, they keep fit, they acquire additional skills such as martial arts or horse riding. They have learned how to value their skills and how to market them, as they've probably already had to find sponsors to pay for their years at RADA. Let's face it, in my day, there were still quite a few, among the girls anyway, whose parents had paid for them, regarding it as a sort of alternative finishing school.

The other way to break into the business then was to go to your local rep and try to get taken on as an A.S.M. This was perfectly possible as you agreed to work for little or no money and there was a great need for willing dogsbodies to do the general running around. But you did manage to land a few small parts which weren't worth the salary of an additional actor for a week's work. If you did well you were likely to progress to bigger roles in due course. With the rep option no longer available today's young hopefuls who don't immediately break into television are left with the alternative of devising their own fringe entertainments in the hope of show-casing their work. They have to find what is now popularly known as a 'space' in which to present their work, and there are so many of these tucked away in such unlikely spots that it is hard to be discovered by an audience, let alone by a questing impresario. No wonder some of them are driven to taking part in the hateful T.V. reality shows where humiliation is partly compensated for by the existence of a very wide, if undiscerning, audience.

Many actors' autobiographies among my contemporaries are full of funny stories about the trials, pressures and inadequacies of life in their repertory days and there is endless scope for these, but the truth is that we were very lucky and,. speaking personally, extremely happy and contented in those far off days.

There were two theatres in which I worked for a longer time than anywhere else. One was the Marlowe Theatre Canterbury, which was weekly rep, and the other was Nottingham Playhouse, both the old and the new, which was fortnightly, and finally became a repertoire company with three to four weeks of rehearsal. My time there was spread intermittently over several years, whereas I stayed at Canterbury for a solid period of almost two years. This much to the disapproval of my agent who had been at school there, and didn't reckon the place much. There were many more prestigious provincial theatre companies but I knew where I was happy and fulfilled. I loved the city itself, then still much damaged by the war and not yet having suffered the total make-over which makes so much of it unrecognisable to me now. There is a new Marlowe Theatre there now, but then it was a converted cinema in the midst of a large car park on land cleared by war damage, with a small pub between the stage door and front-of-house with a very accommodating landlord. On the other side was a small restaurant whose wine waiter was a member of the Guild of Sommeliers and very willing to instruct and develop our palates.

One of our A.S.M.s had parents who owned the Chaucer Hotel, where mine would stay when they travelled, almost every week, from Bedford to see the current play. Mr and Mrs France welcomed all of us from the theatre with great generosity. Another of our A.S.M.s had a father who worked for a chemical company in order to keep his family but whose heart was still in the music world which he had reluctantly abandoned for economic reasons. He was the most gifted accompanist I have ever encountered and regularly played the piano for our musical shows, where his empathic sense of timing meant you worked as one in a comic song. It was he who persuaded me to overcome my uncertainties as to which key I was in and whether the note I was singing was the one I thought it was, and with his encouragement to embark on new and enjoyable voyages of musical discovery. He didn't believe that anybody was naturally tone deaf and, with him at the piano, nobody was. I think his wife disapproved of the amount of time he spent with us but it made him a very happy man. His daughter proved to be a most efficient stage manager and later went into television where she continues to organise everyone and prove to her mother that a lucrative career was a possibility in the field of entertainment.

There were Enid and David at the antique shop, always ready to find us curiosities and beautiful things at a time when such things were affordable, even to us. There were several pubs where both landlord and clientele became great friends and even more in the surrounding countryside, still abounding in hops and fruit. One small free house amongst the fields I remember as 'The Duck' at Pett Bottom. All this, and the wonderful Cathedral, offering rest and refreshment just down the road and livened up on Sundays by the dynamic presence of Dr Hewlett-Johnson, the famous Red Dean. No wonder I knew when I was well off.

And, I was learning my trade in a very well balanced and versatile company, which included my life-long friend, Jean Holness, and the amazing Frank Middlemass, who had been a Major in the war and had a wounded leg, but who never seemed to tire although he was playing leading parts every week. He had a phenomenal memory, a quirky, individual sense of humour and a fund of stories both theatrical and military. He didn't suffer fools gladly and was very suspicious of young, pretty actresses who he felt did not take the theatre seriously. But if he approved of your talents and commitment he was endlessly kind and helpful.

The pattern of work in weekly was Tuesday morning, the blocking of the play: that is working out the moves and technical requirements, entrances and exits etc, and noting these down carefully in the script. The afternoon, after a late lunch, was free for the learning of lines, and then the performance of the current play in the evening. Wednesday morning we worked on Act I – they were pretty well all three-acters in those days – and then the matinee and evening show. Thursday morning we worked on Act II in the morning, and then had the afternoon to learn Act III and the bits of the previous acts we had found difficult or were unsure of. Friday we worked slowly through the whole play, Saturday morning non-stopping run-through, Sunday off to recruit forces and memory and Monday technical and the dress rehearsal and then open in the evening.

After the show on Monday nights we went to the Front-of-House Bar to meet our Playgoers support group for a drink, snacks and a chat. Many of them became close friends and would invite us to their homes whenever we had a spare moment, and their comments were also part of the process of learning. I remember with affection the couple who lived in two converted oast houses, the actress Jessie Evans, who I long admired, and her husband, Donald Bain who lived in a rambling old house in a village nearby, where Jessie was taking time out from her career to give birth to and nurture her daughter, Imogen, and who always welcomed us there. And then there was Frank, disabled and in a wheelchair, and his devoted wife, Brenda. A seat had been removed from the short aisle just inside the side exit doors to make a permanent place for Frank's wheelchair. The couple who were of average education and intelligence came every week without fail and became great connoisseurs and critics over time. It taught me the valuable lesson that constantly playing down to the public and giving them the insubstantial, easy entertainment they are supposed to prefer is not always the best course. Frank confessed to me that he had always enjoyed the light comedies and murder mysteries to begin with, but began to find them much the same. After the performance of "All my Sons" by Arthur Miller he explained that he had enjoyed the play more than any other for a long time. "There seemed to be more to it, somehow" he said.

It was a rigorous and hard-working regime we followed at Canterbury and you wouldn't think that there would be much time to enjoy the delights of the City and the Kent countryside I have described. But we seemed to find time. Jean and I used to take our scripts for learning on the beach at Tankerton to refresh our efforts with a swim, or a walk along the shore for tea at Whitstable. We had our Sundays for visiting, and she, or I at least, would occasionally have the luxury of a 'play out', which meant we were only rehearsing or playing in one week, not both at the same time. This was because plays did not have as many parts for women as for men. I cannot remember poor Frank Middlemass having a play out in the whole two years, though there must have been the odd one. And of course, we all had Canterbury Cricket week free when our theatre was taken over by tradition by the "Old Stagers", a well respected amateur group.

After I had left the company I was recalled in one of these gaps in the summer for amateur production in the year of Shakespeare's quartercentenary by Donald Bain, who was anxious that Marlowe should not be forgotten and who proposed to do a production of "Jew of Malta" with a retired brain surgeon playing the Jew supported by one or two professional players like myself. An interesting experience! And one that produced for me my favourite newspaper critical quote: "Gillian Martell, as a courtesan, was professional on all counts!" Ah well! …….

I first worked in Nottingham on a schools' tour in the nearby towns of Mansfield, Newark and Retford which was organised by the repertory theatre but as a separate company. The play was Andre Obey's "Noah" and I played the lion in an enormous mask. I enjoyed the experience of getting up early and boarding a bus to take us round the various schools. I also met two people who were later to become great friends, Tony Church, the lighting director at the playhouse whose first wife was our stage manager and Henry Livings, the playwright, whose wife was giving us her 'wife of Shem', and who both became life-long friends of mine.

Nottingham paid great attention to its youthful audiences. Apart from these tours, when I joined the company later, under the directorship of Val May, there were six plays in each season for which we performed daily matinees especially for schools amidst much restless giggling from the audience and the inevitable stink bombs let off in the interval to greet us in Act II.

I soon found that fortnightly rep was a much more serious business than weekly. If you have more time it is incumbent upon you to work much harder to produce a higher standard of results. Val May was an imaginative and often inspirational director though a strangely withdrawn man and an extremely tyrannical taskmaster. He had an amazing designer in Voytek, way above the normal repertory standard but sometimes biting off more than the technical resources could chew. This was the old Nottingham Playhouse, once again a converted cinema building but on a much smaller scale backstage than Canterbury had been. The stage door opened directly onto the stage area with just enough wing space for people to walk along it and make an entrance.

On the back wall there was an iron spiral staircase on which it was reputed, someone had once been electrocuted, which wouldn't surprise me in the least given the lack of space for wires and sockets. Underneath the stage there was first a room with a very old boiler in it. Then space for two or three meagre dressing rooms with very thin partitions. You then ascended stairs to the prompt side; where there was a large square space to accommodate prompt desk, lighting board and sound panatrope. There was also sufficient height to accommodate flats and a certain amount of manoeuvrability but not nearly enough for some of the elaborate sets which Voytek conceived to be handled without a great deal of planning, sheer physical effort and tearing of hair by the stage management team. On the back wall was a flight of stairs leading up to the only loo backstage. And woe betide you if you pulled the chain during a performance.

Nothing daunted by this inadequate accommodation Val and Voytek pursued their ambitious programme and, if the actors seldom saw the light of day, the stage management never saw it. What made conditions worse was that the boiler was consistently leaking toxic fumes into our confined space beneath the stage and it was not until yellow smoke started to roll out towards the audience that anything was done about it. There was no shortage of A.S.M.s, for Nottingham was a very prestigious engagement, and they were worked literally to within an inch of their lives. Val wasn't about to engage other actors to play the smaller parts and he had a tendency to do large cast plays so they were frequently doubling minor parts and then when Saturday night came at the end of the fortnight and the actors stumbled home thankfully to their beds they remained in the theatre far into the night doing the 'Get Out' of the current set, only to return on Sunday for the 'Get In' of the next play and a long tedious day helping to erect scenery, to assemble furniture and props and finally to 'stand in', with weary legs, for the lighting director to light the set. Two at least of the young boys developed ulcers and one was removed to hospital with bleeding ulcers. The only female A.S.M., older than the normal run as she had only decided late to enter the profession and go to drama school, became a great friend and when later I sat beside her bed as she was dying of lung cancer in her late forties, I couldn't help thinking of that fatal boiler. However we did really good work in those days at Nottingham, most of the company became household names in later years and he of the bleeding ulcers became a very well respected director and playwright.

The new Nottingham Playhouse which opened in 1963-64 was nevertheless much overdue. Designed by Peter Moro, it is an impressive building but the mind of the architect was still not much taken up with backstage conditions and though there was ample space for storage and manipulation of scenery, and even an impressive revolve to facilitate its employment to maximum effect, there was just a small bare waiting room to act as a green room just inside the stage door, most of the dressing rooms were still below ground with no windows on to the world. The repertoire system of plays which was adopted did give the actors more scope for their personal lives but more time still meant greater efforts towards perfection and a good deal of time was still spent by actors in the troglodyte conditions underground.

John Neville was the director of this new theatre and I spent a great deal of my time in the sixties between his theatre and the Royal Court. John gave me many happy opportunities to play great parts raging from pantomime to Eugene O'Neill's "Long Day's Journey Into Night" playing opposite Robert Ryan, American stunt man and film star and my favourite "Death of a Salesman" by Arthur Miller in which I nearly played opposite Rod Steiger who defaulted on an earlier promise to John, who then took on the role himself. And we both remember it as our finest hour there!

So, as I sit recalling these stirring times and re-capturing so small a part of their essence in writing, I do not envy today's aspiring celebrities and I not even envy the small percentage who 'make it' to the harsh spotlight of the press, the magazines and fickle public. I had a great life, and I knew some wonderful people, some in 'the business', some outside it, but all of them with a genuine interest in, and love of, the theatre. What more could I ask!

PANTOMIMES

I am a sucker for pantomimes. Is it because I adore glitter and bright colours and tinkly tunes and elaborate corny jokes and rituals of audience participation? Is it just because I love Christmas and family outings and children laughing, feeling light hearted and having fun?

Well, that's a lot of the reasons and they're all true. But when I search this increasingly faulty memory of mine I find that this mostly applies to pantomimes I have been to as an adult or performed in myself. Maybe because I grew up in war-time there weren't so many pantomimes about. Two children's shows stand out in my memory and neither could be described as a pantomime. The first is one of those treasures of childhood remembrance which, when recalled, press an immediate button producing a warm glow and a sound like ahhh! But I cannot at this instant recall any details of the plot! I know the heroes and heroines were children and I think there was a dragon and I certainly recall a magical appearance by St George. The play was called, "Where the Rainbow Ends", and it seems to have disappeared with surprising completeness considering its popularity in my youth. I suspect it may be dated, and possibly Jingoistic, but this need not daunt any modern adaptor and producer and I shall really have to mount a crusade to retrieve and revive it.

The second thrilling theatrical event I recall was more obvious: Peter Pan. I know I saw this during the war because my soldier father had kept a letter I wrote to him describing the experience. The pages have 'tick-tock, tick-tock' written all round them as a border and the phrase, "Oh Daddy, they really flew" tells all about my credulity and what really impressed children in that more naïve age.

So pantomimes are perhaps a more recent addiction. And I think they have to be seen just before or soon after Christmas. I am not thinking of the rather tired old commercial pantomimes, which sometimes used to go on into March and became unrecognisable from the original productions, through the terminal boredom of the performers and the reduced receptiveness of an audience getting on with the dreary routine of their working lives. There has to be magic, and you can't create magic every day of the year.

I am thinking more of the old repertory theatre pantomimes with no imported variety artistes who had to fit in their act, and no star refugee from the soaps, uncomfortable, out-of-place and possibly inaudible. No! - A cast of characters drawn from the company of actors with whom the audience were familiar through the year in more serious roles. The rapport between the rep company and their regular audience created just the right atmosphere of warmth and expectation wherein magic may occur. Some surprisingly unexpected skills were displayed and the audience were correspondingly excited, as when a member of their own families suddenly exhibited an unusual talent.

My own initiation into the exciting but rewarding world of pantomime took place at Canterbury rep under the aegis of an imported director who knew all about the subject. She was Pat Sandys, later to become a highly respected T.V. director and producer, and mother of Samantha Bond, that very talented actress, then either a toddler or just a twinkle in her mother's very twinkly eyes – I don't care to reckon up the years!

Pat soon shook us out of our conviction that we knew anything about acting. The level of energy required for any professional performance is something that people not in the profession, and even many amateur actors, find difficult to comprehend. But for a pantomime you can double, or even treble, that. It is not a show in which you draw the audience in to you, it is one in which you push everything out to them – hard. You also speak louder and very clearly. You need to be neat and organised even when appearing chaotic. Even when a character is laid back he needs to demonstrate being laid back rather than actually being so. You don't give an audience a chance to wonder why they are sitting there watching the ridiculous actions of a man in outrageous women's clothes or a girl in tights, slapping her thighs and trying to persuade you that she is a macho being whilst displaying and using all her feminine charms. You and the audience are there to have fun and you all know the rules. And the more fun the actors can have the more the audience is swept with them on a great wave of warmth, laughter and charisma: which is what makes it such a rewarding experience for actors, even twice a day as it usually is over the Christmas period.

The first Christmas at Canterbury I was playing a character called Polly Flinders – goodness knows why. Just an arbitrary name as the pantomime was "Babes in the Wood". I and my partner (I can't remember what he was called: Wee Willie Winkie probably!) were there as the comic juveniles, mirroring the antics of the two leads and conducting our own strange love affair alongside them. The local ballet school, who always like to join the rep at Christmas, provided the ballet of leaves to cover up the Babes. They also performed a hula-hoop, cha-cha-cha number, and I was elected to join them for this – right in the middle of the front row of course. All the young girls had become remarkably proficient with these alarming hoops even though they had only just come back "in" – you have to be topical in panto – and of course they showed me up horribly. Thank goodness when you're playing a comedy character you can always pretend you were meant to drop the thing, but I felt the children rather despised me. Or perhaps it was just pity.

An actress friend of mine who was very petite and athletic made rather a speciality of playing animals and as her family lived in Canterbury, and she liked to come home for Christmas, she had been playing cats or geese, or whatever, every year in the panto and was a rather charming little dog in "Babes in the Wood". Well, you've got to have a dog in a wood haven't you? – All those trees.

However the following year when we did Aladdin, she went on strike. She said she was tired of being animals and wanted to play the Princess. Our director saw the force of her argument and agreed. As the part of the Empress was filled by an older member of the company he hadn't an appropriate role for me. "Would you like to be the animal?" he said, "the children ought to have their animal." I wasn't at all as large as I am now, but I was not known for my athletic qualities. "What sort of animal could I possibly be?" I demurred. "Well, it is China," he said, "How about a Giant Panda?" And a Giant Panda I duly became – the trusted friend of Wishee Washee – and ambassador to all the children in the audience. The trouble was that at that time it proved impossible to find and hire a Panda costume. Finally, somebody was found who agreed to make one and she didn't do at all a bad job. Visually the costume was as convincing as these things need to be. The trouble was that, not being a theatrical person, the helpful costume-maker had not envisaged that I would be spending a certain amount of time off stage and might like the use of my hands, and indeed might require to at least partially remove part of the costume to attend to certain bodily functions, like eating, drinking, peeing, breathing, and mopping up my sweat. The costume was warm and the action at times quite energetic and I consequently sweated a great deal. We did what we could to ease the immediate breathing and visual problems and our dear stage manager spent the entire run with boxes of tissues in the wings rubbing me down as best he could. The wardrobe mistress was also required to stand by with a needle and thread for hasty running repairs to my seams when I had been particularly active on stage. A highlight of this year, I remember, was a skiffle group in which I, as the Panda, somehow played the washboard with my unwieldy paws.

My favourite moment in the performance was when several of us were required to appear at the back of the audience shouting and causing a commotion making our way towards the stage while I, as the dear little animal, was supposed to attempt to sit on people's knees. I quickly abandoned the idea of attempting to plant my several stones on to the laps of eager children, but kept a look out for any stalwart fathers in the audience who seemed to me to be up to the challenge. The old Marlowe Theatre Canterbury was a converted cinema and had no pass door to the auditorium and we were thus compelled to exit the stage door and walk through the car park to the front of house. At the corner of the car park on our way was our friendly neighbourhood pub, "Jock's". Jock used to have a row of drinks lined up for us and we just had time to down them before making our appearance in the auditorium. The regulars got quite used to seeing the Emperor and Empress of China, Wishee Washee and one flagging Giant Panda, standing at the bar every night. In spite of my exertions and discomfort I enjoyed Aladdin very much. The time-honoured custom of playing jokes and changing the performance on the last night of the panto was much enjoyed in towns with repertory theatres. A lot of people booked twice so that they would know what the show was supposed to be like, and then came to enjoy seeing what their actor friends got up to on the last night. In this production, I recall, Aladdin had just been shut in the cave by his wicked uncle and was bemoaning the fact that he was all alone under the ground and would never see a human soul again, when Wishee Washee crossed from one side of the stage to the other muttering "They said follow the green light for Paddington but I don't know ...."

Much later I was asked by John Neville to go and do pantomime at Nottingham. With much mirth between him and my agent they decided I should play the Fairy Godmother – a most unlikely and possibly malicious thought. It follows that it was very important to me who was playing my Demon King. Now, the Fairy Godmother and Demon King, or their equivalent, are somewhat apart from the rest of the cast. They alone do not have a change of costume for the walk down – being immortals they are above that sort of consideration. This makes them very handy for doing the front-cloth scene, immediately before the grand finale, while everyone else is changing, including the set. They usually work on the apron anyway, and almost work exclusively with each other, only appearing occasionally in the main action, often accompanied by a flash and a puff of smoke. If there are openings on to the forestage or apron which are below the curtain line they use these and, by tradition, the Good Fairy always enters O.P. - which is audience left, stage right. If she doesn't it is bad luck. My Demon King turned out to be an old friend, Harold Innocent, a man of imposing dimensions, a strong personality, and a powerful singing voice. But he was also the very Queen of Camp, and was known affectionately as the "Diva" – a nickname which referred equally to his singing voice and to his temperament - with a capital 'T'.

As he was wont to display his feminine side so forcefully, I knew that I couldn't top him there, and so I decided that I would also play my fairy as a complete Narcissist, in love with her own beauty and power. I was helped in this decision by the design for my costume – pure gold and spangles with a very bouffant skirt, and my wig – a riot of golden curls that had John Neville addressing me as 'Bubbles'. I also drew inspiration from a line I had to Jack, "Think beautiful thoughts and I will appear." (The play was Jack in the Beanstalk, by the way.) Add to all this a longer pair of false eyelashes than I had ever worn, a vivid make up, and I was equipped for battle. And of course you do have the wand! With both of us playing our roles with supreme egotism, instead of as a double act it seemed strangely to work, in the event. For our front-cloth number Harold sang "I can't give you anything but love, baby", with me sending him up and pointing out where all the love was actually going. As I never usually had the chance to play glamorous roles I rather enjoyed myself. But my image of myself as a beauty was somewhat defeated by John Neville's four year old in the audience one night. In the thick of the dramatic action he felt he hadn't seen me for a while and asked his mother about it. She pointed to the door from which I usually appeared and said, "She's in her little house." He nodded wisely and said, "I expect she's on the loo."

I decided to take my own two children to the pantomime early in life. It was Cinderella at Richmond and I took my son to the evening performance where his happiest moment was that he was able to grab one of the bags of sweets that were thrown into the audience. After the show I was able to take him to meet Roy Kinnear, an old friend of mine who was playing Buttons. Roy loved children and was very funny but my son was struck completely dumb. I think he enjoyed himself. Later I took my daughter to a matinee as she was not quite three. She like me adores glitter and pretty dresses, so she was happy, though I don't know how much of the plot she understood, as I heard her afterwards telling a friend "and the two naughty sisters wouldn't let Cinderella have her ball back. You shall go to the ball!" Fortunately the singer playing Cinderella was also an acquaintance of mine so I took my daughter backstage to meet her. We were expected but as there is not much time to go out and eat between the shows Sheila White had already changed when we got to her dressing room. She very sweetly showed my daughter some of the clothes and props and chatted to her gaily, although Ilona was very quiet. Then as we all went down the stairs together she said, "Mummy, when can we see Cinderella?" Sheila stopped dead and said "Oh dear! Just a minute!" Then, bless her, she ran upstairs and soon came down again, wearing her dress and wig and speaking in her stage voice she said, "My friend said you wanted to meet me. I am Cinderella!" And a great smile spread over my daughter's face. At that moment, perhaps, a costume designer was born, and my daughter has never since accepted less than the real thing.

LIGHT ENTERTAINMENT

I was watching a TV show the other day about the story of light entertainment and how so many of the performers ended up hosting games shows after the Variety Theatres round the country closed. The merciless exposure of television made it impossible to keep doing the same old act and difficult to find ever-new material. And I realised that when I made my debut in the theatre in 1956 I was in on the dying fall of an era that had begun with music hall, had spawned Charlie Chaplin and sent him off into film land, had filled large, ornate Variety Theatres round the country and had even included seaside shows on the end of the pier and later in holiday camps.

Television had already begun to make its inroads on the comic talent and invention of this most volatile and precarious branch of "Show Business". I was privileged to have witnessed the inspired genius of Freddie Frinton, captured in those early days of TV but live, I presume, and not enshrined on tape. He had two famous scenes that rivalled anything the Marx Brothers could produce at their best. As impossible to explain his visual gags as theirs. It is all in the personality and the timing. In one scene he was a doddery waiter serving single-handedly a long table of unseen guests, slyly swigging the wine as he trotted round and sinking further and further into a strangely dignified drunkenness. In another he was involved with a set of invisible dancers performing "The Lancers" and being jerked suddenly into frenzied activity by unseen hands. As I say it is impossible to describe.

By the time I left RADA and embarked on my career there were still plenty of variety shows on television, including the infamous "Black and White Minstrel Show" which my father loved, in spite of being virtually tone deaf, because he loved to hear all the old songs, perhaps all the more because he couldn't reproduce them! There were several double acts about in those days including Bill Maynard and Terry Scott and Jewel and Warriss, who were taking part in the Vic Oliver Show when I was invited to appear briefly and be interviewed about my recent award of the RADA Bancroft Gold Medal. I was very shy and unsure of myself in those days and completely bewildered by the loud, confident, totally professional people surrounding me. I had been visited in the dressing room by a gentleman who said I had to join Equity instantly (as a probationary member in those days until you had done 42 weeks work) which of course I was glad to do but I could have done without him at that moment. During the rehearsal run-through the interviewer had told me a couple of questions he would ask, but when it came to the actual show, having introduced me he just baldly said, "Well Gillian and what does this medal mean?" Whereupon, thoroughly unnerved by the glitter around me and the leering attentions of the sleazy Ben Warriss I simply gulped and stammered, "Well, it doesn't mean much really." End of interview; Parkie would have despaired of me.

Another outcome of the medal and the "Public Show" at RADA was that I was contacted by about four different agents, one of which being my dear friend Peter Crouch who became my agent and never gave me any reason to wish to change in 41 years. But the most frightening interview came about through the father of a school-friend, John Bancroft, who ran the Variety Theatre at Peterborough where I remember seeing a very young and nervous Tommy Steele. I had become friendly with the whole family, particularly the older daughter, who was at that time working in the box-office of Bertram Mills Circus and was later on the management team of Sadlers Wells Theatre which became the English National Opera at the Coliseum. Bancroft père thought he'd give me a good start by recommending me to an agent in glowing terms. I trotted along to my appointment and found myself in a room with both Lou and Leslie Grade who had not yet created their TV empire but were very well known agents indeed and were rather stymied by the lack of pizzazz of this very unimpressive, shy ex-student. They did their best to oblige their friend Mr Bancroft by being very genial – I can't remember if I was offered a cigar, they were certainly each smoking one – but they failed to see how they could help me. I found it very unnerving – all these variety people were so much larger than life.

In my early days in repertory I was to share digs with some of them, particularly in Nottingham where the old Empire theatre stood alongside the Royal, which took, and still does, the No 1 touring dates. So close indeed were these two theatres that their stage doors faced each other across a narrow alley way and legend goes that a magician's assistant having been magically 'vanished' from the Empire stage re-appeared at the back of the stalls at the Royal during a straight play shouting "Here I am!". I have since played the newly refurbished Royal when on tour but the but the Empire has long ago vanished itself along with a lovely left over British restaurant café next door where they used to do a great Welsh Rarebit.. In my early days at the Playhouse I shared digs with the cheerfully vulgar Jimmy James and his equally famous 'stooge' whose name nobody ever remembers. He was an extremely tall, thin gawky man with a fairly ugly face whose lugubrious features never cracked into the smallest smile as Jimmy James verbally abused him, twice nightly to the great glee of the audience. He appeared to be a total idiot on stage but was actually a very shrewd fellow, who did very well on the horses I believe. I remember now, his name is Eli Woods. I met the pair in Nottingham and in Coventry where the great Sam Newsome kept the Hippodrome alive and successful long after other provincial variety houses had closed. Some great friends that I met in both places and I believe also at Ipswich were a strange quartet which consisted of the Miles twins (Pauline and Estelle) and the Cox twins (male) to whom they were married. The Cox twins were the comedians whilst the Miles twins were mainly decorative in the act I think. They seemed to get plenty of work. I was never quite sure that they were too particular about who was married to which and I think they told me that it didn't really matter as they were all good friends together. As I rider to this I have since watched a further episode of the TV Light Entertainment programme and lo and behold up popped the self same Cox twins, long haired and raddled looking, speaking turn about or in unison as always and cheerfully bemoaning the fact that rock and roll had killed variety – no mention of their wives. I wonder what happened to them.

I see from an old scrapbook my parents urged me to keep but which was long ago abandoned, that there is a review of my earliest TV performance of Chekhov's "The Proposal" for which I had won the aforementioned medal and which we then repeated on live television (scary). This crit. consists of one line stating that our production was a gem. The rest of the space is taken up with slating Bill Maynard for his efforts in the TV show "Great Scott, It's Maynard" complaining that he must stop laughing at his own jokes.

This vividly brings back to me working with him in a play by Henry Livings at the new Nottingham Playhouse. He had long since broken up with terry Scott and was trying his hand a straight acting, including giving his "Bottom" in "The Dream". He was very exhausting to be with off-stage as his conversation was a string of jokes each one punctuated with a laugh and a "Boom-Boom" in the manner of Basil Brush. He was quite a family man however and invited us all over to Leicester, where he lived, one evening during rehearsals to attend a performance of his son's rock band. Joan Littlewood came to watch a rehearsal, invited by Henry, and was instantly captivated by Bill's brash, larger than life personality. Just the sort of raw material she delighted in. It was quite tricky dealing with him on stage as, although he was quite professional, he did have a tendency to ad-lib given a little encouragement – or none at all. However we got on all right and it wasn't as bad, I am reliably informed, as working with Spike Milligan who was apt to write a whole new play as he went along on certain nights when the mood took him.

A strange, forceful, confident, vulnerable breed – the Variety Artiste. I am glad that I was able to catch the tail end of their greatest era before they metamorphosed into game show hosts and gave way to today's brand of, equally brave, stand-up comedians.

FOR JEAN

Written and read by me at her funeral

I first met Jean in 1958, when I joined Canterbury Repertory theatre as a pretty raw recruit and found her already enthroned as leading actress and darling of the entire town. She immediately adopted me as a daughter and invited me into her own special world of theatre, the pub, animals, swimming and the crossword. I used to help her a bit with this last but she was much quicker and better than I. However, once I got an answer to a clue which she didn't know.

"It's Bugaboo" I said. Jean said

"Nonsense, there's no such word. You're thinking of bugbear." So I had to prove it to her with a dictionary and ever after, that is what she called me - Bugaboo!

She introduced me to my first Bloody Mary and was not at all shaken, as I was, when a few minutes later a lady walked into the pub with a baby gorilla in her arms. Jean explained that she was a member of the Aspinall family who kept a private zoo and the gorilla was in fact real and not a figment of my drunken imagination. We were to see it there, at the Olive Branch, on many later occasions, until it grew older and one day grabbed the landlord by the collar across the bar and was subsequently barred.

Immediately opposite the Olive Branch was the magnificent Canterbury Cathedral where Jean and I would often go to Evensong to marvel at the superior theatrical talents displayed in his sermons by Dr Hewlett-Johnson, the Red Dean.

We would often go to learn our lines on the beach at Tankerton, where Jean would improve my swimming skills between scenes. Born and bred on the Isle of Wight, Jean was herself a very strong swimmer. When still in their teens, she and her friend became the first women to swim the Solent, a notoriously difficult and dangerous stretch of water, with her father in the rowing boat that accompanied them. If the war hadn't intervened, she would have had a go at the Channel.

She was also the cox of a hefty police four, rowing in the sea at Ryde. They won many cups and Jean had a gold watch the policemen had inscribed with their names and presented to her which she was very proud of.

Jean was a very versatile actress and I have photographs of her looking incredibly glamorous and many others where she gleefully appeared looking hideous or comic. She could play any age, employ any accent, and make you laugh or make you cry. Canterbury loved her, and when she finally tore herself away to give London the benefit of her talents, the pub next door to the theatre was bursting at the seams with her friends and admirers for her farewell party. Jock, the landlord, had applied for an extension to his licensing hours and the magistrate had said

"Oh for Jean, of course. Granted." Some time after the extended closing time with hilarity within and light streaming out into the car park, a young policeman suddenly put his head round the door and a hush fell. The embarrassed bobby stammered

"Oh sorry! I just came to say goodbye to Jean!"

Our friendship continued in London and she eventually became a much loved godmother to my daughter whom Jean, always unselfish, would not have wished to be here today, as she is on her honeymoon.

Jean never did much television because she didn't really feel happy unless she was setting out for a theatre every night and being part of a company. She got waylaid into doing a lot of understudying and her room or the adjacent wardrobe would become the focus of many happy little drinking and socialising clubs. After the show she would usually repair to the Players Theatre where her social life could continue in the ambience and with the people she loved. Amongst others, she understudied Margaret Lockwood, Coral Browne, Wendy Hiller and Rachel Kempson and became great friends with them. Although she did, quite often play for them, it seemed a bit of a waste of her talents, but the trouble was she was so reliable and such a help with learning their lines and such fun to be with that they kept asking for her and she could never resist a theatre opportunity. So she was constantly in work and very happy trotting off nightly to her preferred environment.

In her later years and when she was finally unable to work, it made even more time for the animals in her life. Her dogs were usually rescue cross-breeds, from Joxer who was of the terrier persuasion to the vaguely corgi, Charlie. She even landed me with a puppy from a litter she had watched being born. The only aristocrat she had was a very beautiful, superior longhaired Persian cat, Guinness, who lived to be twenty under her loving care and she was so called because she was black and because she had been given to her by Alec Guinness. When she could no longer keep pets, she made do with the squirrels in the park, who would actually sit on her lap to take nuts; her special duck, who came when she called and whose leg had been severely mauled by a fox; the donkey she had adopted and sent money for, called Rosie; and the birds who came to her windowsill.

Jean was generous, fiercely independent and fantastically loyal. She made and kept great friends who repaid her loyalty in her last illness and made it more bearable for her. She would want me to mention Fiona and Cookie.

I have a photograph of her and me in my room, taken when we did a revue at Canterbury. I am in beret, scarf and glasses, holding a placard reading "Down with the H bomb". She is in an elderly, flowered dress with a cloche hat and holding a bunch of very wilted wayside flowers. I took it to show her the last time I saw her in hospital and in a whisper she sang

"We've come all the way from Aldermaston, Aldermaston, Aldermaston." I had sung then:

"We've made it now, I'm pleased to say" and Jean had held up her wilted bouquet and sung

"I'm glad we came the pretty way!"

Well, Jean, you have made it now, and I'm glad that, on the whole, and often together, we did come the pretty way.

On behalf of all your friends I salute you here with your favourite word:

Jean - Cheers!

THE ROYAL COURT THEATRE

My agent once sent me a first night telegram (when such things still existed) reading "You have spent more time at the Royal Court than most Queens have." It was certainly one of the busiest, most productive and possibly happiest times of my life. I first joined the company in 1965 soon after the theatre had been taken over following the death of the legendary George Devine, by a triumvirate consisting of Bill Gaskill, Iain Cuthbertson and Keith Johnstone. Bill Gaskill soon emerged as the overall and eventually the sole artistic director. Iain was basically an actor and gave a very fine performance as Sergeant Musgrave in the fourth play of the season, when I joined the company. He did act for a time as the voice of common sense and restraint to the headstrong Mr Gaskill. I was never quite sure about what Keith Johnstone was doing. It was mostly his own thing, and with masks.

It was a new thing for this theatre to support a permanent company doing plays in repertoire and, though the plays were exciting, the direction good and the company mainly young and vital, it didn't work. The stark truth was that to be financially viable the theatre needed to be able to transfer its successes to the West End theatre where prices and numbers of seats were more realistic. With a repertoire system and a company of actors tied to the Royal Court this was obviously not possible. The company was officially disbanded in under a year but by then Bill had laid the foundations for a group of people sympathetic to his ideas and methods of working. It was a group that he drew on ever after, whilst we were obviously and necessarily free to accept other work and he was free to add the requisite big names to the mix as and when the plays required it.

But the Royal Court always had been, and should be, a place of discovery, trial and encouragement for new, unknown authors and as such it provided the most exciting times of my professional life. I was more than a little scared of working with Bill Gaskill who was a born teacher even more than he was a director and was very rigorous in his training of actors and his relentless way of pushing them to the limits of their ability in his attempts to unlock the potential he could see in them. He would even sacrifice his directorial responsibilities in a specific attempt to develop some aspect of a particular actor's progress. I knew also that he favoured improvisation as one method of attaining his goals and this was not a process that appealed to me. I am an interpreter of other people's writing and, according to testimonials I have from certain authors, a faithful and sympathetic one. I do not relish improvisation as I find that one's self is bound to intrude and my self is a very non-confident and self conscious self. I cannot hold onto and explore my character nearly as well as I can with his own words to speak.

In fact, so anxious was I when I first joined the company for "Sergeant Musgrave's Dance" that I had a vivid dream one night of Iain Cuthbertson, huge and looming in his scarlet sergeant's tunic, holding out to me a cup of blood and saying, "Go on, drink it up Gillian, we all drink it here."

I soon became absorbed in the company however, and found my own ways of dealing with methods of working I had not before encountered. And there were other directors with whom I was initially more comfortable. Jane Howell, whom I had worked with at Hornchurch and at Coventry and who first invited me to the Court for Musgrave, for which I am eternally grateful to her. And Peter Gill who had been A.S.M. at Nottingham when I was there, warm and Welsh and mischievous, formidably intelligent and articulate and now proving to be as good a director as he was a fresh and interesting playwright. These knew my work as I knew theirs and helped ease me eventually into a relationship with Bill Gaskill which was – I won't say happy, because you could never rest on your laurels with him – but always stimulating and finally deeply satisfying.

And then there were the authors: Arnold Wesker who I felt was at a rather anxious stage in his career after the early success of his trilogy which included the incomparable "Roots". He had written a somewhat didactic play designed basically to show where the trade union movement had gone wrong after a magnificent start and was entitled "Their very own and Golden City", which might give you pause for a start. It took place in Durham and whilst the two main characters, played by myself and Ian McKellan, aged considerably throughout the play, we had to keep returning throughout the plot to scenes in Durham Cathedral on one day of our extreme aspiring youth. This entailed incidentally my one and only attempt at a Geordie accent, but also initially two other actors playing us while young. This was deemed in rehearsal not to work and we were condemned to play ourselves throughout, which created considerable problems as to costume, wigs and make-up. With some of the changes it felt as if we were doing revue. This was not a good feeling as Arnold was deadly serious about the piece which was over-long and wavered between a sentimental idealism, which was rather uncomfortable, and out and out political lectures which were even more so, particularly when it was decreed that we should give an 11 a.m. performance specifically to an audience of trade union leaders who were as unwilling to be there as we were. Dear Arnold, I loved him for his enthusiasm and revered him for a great deal of his work and I found him friendly and helpful at rehearsals, but his gratitude to us for our performances made me feel uncomfortable, no matter that I strained to do the best work I could, because I felt that my heart wasn't in the same place that his was and I was sorry for it.

There were many other authors I had a chance to talk to and work with, notably David Cregan who became a great friend after I first worked with him on a Sunday night performance of his play "The Dancers", when there were horrendous technical difficulties and we never did get through a dress rehearsal and consequently played the whole piece on a great burst of adrenalin from nerves, myself being hampered by an enormously padded costume into which I was sewn with no possibility of going to the loo throughout. I later did a television play of David's in Derbyshire where he had been married and I met his wife and family. We had to be taken up to very high peaks to film in a four-wheel drive and I learned from the result an added theatrical truth – never work with children, animals - or beautiful scenery. You can never win.

There was Chris Hampton, quiet and intellectual and a good friend with whom I was later to go to Canada, and who provided me with one of those outstanding memories as he invited me to accompany him and Bill Gaskill to drinks one evening at the flat of the legendary Peggy Ramsay, his agent, about whom Simon Callow has written, a play entitled "Peggy for You".

But of course, the first and foremost playwright, whose works I performed at the Royal Court was Edward Bond. Not necessarily first and foremost in overall importance although I think he is pretty special, but first and foremost in my life. So much that I think he deserves a chapter all on his own. I've gone on too long now anyway.

EDWARD BOND

When I first arrived at the Royal Court Theatre in 1965 the first three plays of the new season had just gone into the repertoire and the one which was causing the most interest with the critics and indeed the newspapers generally was Edward Bond's play "Saved". One of his plays had had a Sunday night performance at the Court a year or so earlier but this was his first to have a proper run. Edward had very definite and radical views about the theatre and its purpose and indeed about modern society in general and he believed that change in one could help to bring about change in the other. He had no use for frivolous or light drama or even for classical plays, especially at the Court. He believed they should concentrate on the works of young, committed playwrights with something of value to say about our modern world and a fresh and dynamic way of saying it. He called Shakespeare 'the Great Bourgeois". He was a socialist, naturally, and a man who had at the same time a deep basic love of and pity for the human race and a sharp and obsessive awareness of its failings and cruelties. I always felt that he had an abnormally thin skin with all his nerves tingling at the surface but that he also possessed a suit of armour to provide a necessary barrier between him and the world. He wasn't easy to get to know initially and he would be enigmatic and unhelpful at rehearsals yet when Bill Gaskill had reduced one or other of us to his usual pulp Edward's sympathy was ready and genuine. I became very close to him and to his wife, Elizabeth, a most warm and charming Austrian lady who we first got to know when touring Edward's plays on the continent.

I sat through the performance of "Saved" knowing nothing of Edward at the time, rigid and aching with the concentration that goes with complete involvement. I didn't know whether I really liked it or not or could ever bear to sit through it again, but I knew it was something completely different and that I had at certain points been unusually moved and enlightened. Afterwards I became aware of the great furore there had been in the papers about the scene where two or three youths, out of idleness, boredom and peer pressure, threw stones at a baby in a pram. A shocking scene of course, especially back then, but what I found even more shocking was that the young mother, who had abandoned the pram for a short while to pursue her own trivial and self absorbed ends, returned at the end of the scene and wheeled off her child, talking to it soothingly but, still self –absorbed and self-pitying, without noticing that there was anything wrong. Her cooing litany as she walked slowly off, bending over the pram and slightly rocking it, was all about herself. The scenes within the family were equally sharp, perceptive and ironic. It was quite an introduction to a major new playwright.

The first play of his that I was in was "Narrow Road to the Deep North", taking place in a province of Japan ruled by a tyrant in the seventeenth century and the protagonist was the real life Haiku poet Matsuo Basho who took the Narrow Road in search of enlightenment at the beginning of the play. He was as enigmatic and cryptic as his verse and at the end of the play returned after many years having come up with the Japanese equivalent of the answer 42! Meanwhile the main body of the play features the tyrant Shogo and his atrocities; the Buddhist priest Kiro whose answer is finally to commit hara kiri; and the English brother and sister played by Nigel Hawthorne and myself in anachronistic Victorian costume so that we could embody Edward's favourite despised bourgeois values. We were incidentally more tyrannical than the tyrant but in the nicest possible way explaining 'its all for your own good' to the natives. Quite the usual Bond mix and wonderfully satisfying to play. Nigel was his usual urbane, posh-spoken silly ass with the steel underneath half-hidden and I, in full crinoline and Salvation Army bonnet also had a ball with a nice little tambourine to bang at will. One of the dramatic moments of the play is when Kiro, who has put a sacred vase on his head when larking about with other young monks, and is stuck in it, asks Shogo, the tyrant, for help in removing it. The monks have tried everything to ease it off but Shogo, who has no use for religion, simply calls for a hammer and breaks the pot. The pots we used were carefully pre-cracked by the stage management so that they would fall apart at a tap, but one matinee Jack Shepherd got a little carried away and managed to hit Ken Cranham's head. As the blood began to trickle down from under the bald wig all the monks wore, Jack Shepherd stepped forward and announced, "This actor is hurt and must go to hospital." Poor Ken was carted away and his understudy, James Hazeldine, who was fortunately playing another monk and was therefore on stage at the time and dressed identically to Ken, nervously took over for the rest of the show. We were all rather shaken (for it was quite a heavy hammer) and somewhat subdued, but during the evening show Ken Cranham appeared briefly in the wings grinning and showing off his bandages. James acquitted himself very well and Ken was soon back in the performance.

The second Edward Bond play I was involved in was called "The Sea" and was a different kettle of fish altogether. Whilst it still contained the 'messages' so dear to Edward's heart and also its fair share of weird, complicated characters, it was much lighter in tone and contained some very funny scenes. One of these was the rehearsal of a play by a group of earnest, well-bred, amateur ladies. It was set in the Edwardian era and I played a companion to Coral Brown's lady of the manor, a typically vague, repressed ineffectual spinster with a redeeming streak of gentle, stubborn malice. It was a gift of a role and in a characteristically strange Bond scene of a funeral with a piano on a cliff-top, we all had to sing "for those in peril on the sea" before casting forth the ashes. I had already ruined the dowager's funeral oration by searching in my large handbag and muttering to myself, but intentionally audible, a monologue of vague complaints and doubts as to whether I had performed certain duties or not. I then crowned my offence by soaring into a reedy solo descant in the hymn, in apparent total religious fervour and oblivious to those around me. It had originally been intended that Coral would sing a base line harmony at this point but this she had felt unable to do. I knew that I could produce the right thin soprano however and can, if carefully taught, just manage to hold onto a simple harmonic line. Coral's outrage at my character's performance contributed greatly and generously to the round of applause which stopped the show every night. This is at the same time gratifying and worrying, as one feels obliged to produce the same effect nightly. Fortunately I managed this, aided by the fact that we had unusually full houses. The play had caught on due to critical appreciation and word-of-mouth and quite a lot of actors came to see it. For obvious reasons, I enjoyed it hugely and in this country it is the one of his works most often performed although on the continent, where

Edward's reputation is greater than here, his darker plays are generally preferred.

My third Bond play was different again, and rewarding in another way. It was called "Bingo" and featured John Gielgud as Shakespeare and Arthur Lowe as Ben Johnson. I played Shakespeare's daughter Judith, a shrewish and disappointed character whom I found very difficult to play. Bill Gaskill called in to watch a rehearsal and gave me the note, 'A little less Brecht and a little more Stanislavski, Gillian.' The play was an exploration of a playwright's life and work and Edward was more than usually enigmatic at rehearsals. Hard though I found the role it was a great privilege for me as well as a valuable experience and eventually a joy, to play scenes with Gielgud. He was always kind and helpful and when the run started he asked his chauffeur to drive me home to Primrose Hill at night. The first time this happened his chauffeur said to me, "I thought you'd like a ride in the Rolls but as I leave it in the underground garage at Park Lane at night, would you mind if I picked my own car up there to take you on? It would save me going back." Of course I said I didn't mind. I was thankful to avoid the tube after a hard evening and had no-one I particularly wished to impress. "Bingo" was a great experience although I am not sure I fully understand the play.

I was to do one more of his plays some years later, tempted briefly away from my maternal responsibilities by the knowledge of a good Mother's Help at home and the fact that it was Bond. This was a play called "The Fool" about the rural poet, John Clare, played beautifully by Tom Courtenay. Edward Bond himself wrote poetry and used Clare to illustrate his usual themes and pre-occupations. I played a totally demented Mary Lamb and wandered through the production clutching a large tapestry cloak bag with wooden handles, referred to always, mysteriously and importantly as 'the ornamental bag.' I kept it for years after until it fell apart. I remember a very enjoyable scene at the close of the piece, playing chess in an asylum with John Normington dressed as Napoleon. Our crazy cross-talk was probably full of meaning as Edward believes the insane are sane and vice versa. Clare himself was deemed mad in later life.

So, there it is: a catalogue of horrors, fears, tragedies and injustices, interlaced with sometimes bitter humour – all from that quiet, passionate, cynical but ultimately caring person that is Edward Bond.

MACBETH (SH! DON'T MENTION IT)

As I think I have indicated, Bill Gaskill had his own very definite ideas about theatre and was fairly contemptuous of the opinions of critics and even of the average audience.

During his time at the Royal Court he had some memorable battles with the critics, at one point actually banning them from the theatre; not to mention his struggles with the Lord Chamberlain pre 1968 when this gentleman made his exit, thus obviating the need for Sunday performance as a club theatre and heralding the birth of the Theatre Upstairs as a means of trying out the more experimental dramas.

It was not surprising then, that when Bill came to do a production of Macbeth in 1966 his concept of the play was not just controversial but, some might say, perverse. He explained to us at the read-through that the play was chock-full of the most graphic images of darkness, both actual and symbolic, reflecting the moral content of the piece, and that he therefore proposed to present the play in a bright sandpaper yellow box set, which would be flooded with light. It was up to the actors, he informed us, to create the darkness in the minds of the audience. He further compounded his contrariness by casting three black actors as the witches and in a final wayward fancy, getting them to double as the hired murderers.

He had, of necessity, secured for himself a really strong Macbeth in the shape of Alec Guinness. His Lady M was also a very strong choice, and a brave one, because this was Simone Signoret whose English as she had proved in many films was excellent, but who had never before faced the challenge of Mr Shakespeare's verse. This proved to be more of a stumbling block than we anticipated. Dear Gordon Jackson did sterling work both on and off stage as Banquo, Maurice Roeves was MacDuff, my good friend Susie Engel his Lady, and I was the only other female, not a witch, the Gentlewoman in the sleepwalking scene. I had very much wanted to do this as I am a great admirer of Simone Signoret and also of her husband, Yves Montand, both of whom I had been privileged to see in Paris in a translation of Arthur Miller's "The Crucible", "Les Sorcières de Salem".

So I started rehearsals in a very eager frame of mind, finding Simone as friendly and charming as I had hoped, enveloped as she always was in a gentle mist of "Shalimar" perfume which still recalls her to me nostalgically. And yes, I did get to meet Yves Montand, to lose my hand in his enormous one and to experience his warm sexy charisma. Indelible memories, those.

The play however, was not going well. Alec Guinness had naturally been working on his role for some time and had presumably settled on the broad outlines with Bill Gaskill. He had opted to use a Scottish accent, which we discovered at the read through, and had all hastily to follow suit. Simone, on the other hand, whilst I am sure she had been reading the part over and over and practising her English, needed all the help she could get. Unfortunately she was not the sort of woman that Bill found it easy to communicate with, with her strong feisty femininity, of which I think he was a little afraid. He did not feel able to browbeat her and was unable to find a channel to connect with her as rehearsal methods were different in France, so he tended to leave her rather on her own. Gordon Jackson was a great help to her here, as he had worked with her in films and was able to keep up her spirits and to interpret Bill to her when possible. Susie Engel and I were at one in our admiration of her and a familiarity with French theatre, and I think we helped her too to feel more at home. Meanwhile Bill was correspondingly hard on those of us that he knew well and drove us mercilessly to speak the wonderful poetry that is Macbeth well enough to create the images he had in mind for the audience. But audiences do not suspend their visual faculties, however beautiful the sound and intense the actors' interpretations. Their eyes received a further assault besides the brilliantly lit set when the costumes were revealed to be of a uniform grey, homespun looking material of uninspiring shape, Simone indeed appearing in an enormous grey tent.

The three black actors too, were hardly proving a homogeneous element. Zakes Mokae was from America and had a certain sophistication which Femi Euba, from South Africa, rougher and younger, did not appreciate. And Jomoke Debayo, the sole female witch, was from Lagos very proud of being Yuroba, with a family involved in government and her own radio show back home and obviously considered herself a much higher caste and so ignored the other two completely. I got to know her better than the others as we three women were sharing a dressing room and I must say she was very friendly with Susie and me, and we enjoyed some very tasty African food in her family flat in Maida Vale.

We opened to an expected castigation from the critics over the somewhat unusual production. Guinness received a due measure of praise but poor Simone was treated in an unnecessarily harsh manner. It was true that she had not won the battle with the Bard's language but her characterisation was strong and I felt very keenly in the sleep walking scene the truth and power of her emotions. It was a very shaken Lady M who stood in the wings on the second night waiting for her entrance. She had said that it reminded her of the old story, "Simone Signoret is going to play Lady Macbeth". Voice from the stalls: "She's a whore!" "Nevertheless ......". As she stepped forward towards the stage she whispered to the two of us who were waiting with her for solidarity, "Nevertheless...". She acquitted herself very well but we could all imagine what she was going through and were astonished therefore when after the curtain call, Sir Alec rounded on her irritably and accused her very noisily of clinging to his arms too hard. It was an ugly moment. The following evening we learned from her that, as the two of them were in their dressing rooms preparing, much earlier than the rest of us, he had come into her room and apologised for his outburst adding, "But you see what I had to put up with." He showed her his arms covered in bruises. She was naturally devastated, especially in her vulnerable state, and was stammering her regrets when he said "Ha-ha!" and rubbed at his arms where he had incredibly taken the trouble and time to produce these realistic bruises with makeup. We could not believe he could be so insensitive to her distressed state, but Gordon Jackson told us it was just like him. They had been on a film together where Sir Alec had reduced a new, very young make-up artist to tears by commanding her to remove his moustache and shouting at her for her clumsiness, when in actual fact it was his own moustache he had grown for the part. He invited a party of us to dinner at his house where we spent a somewhat uncomfortable evening. Conversation did not flourish in the uneasy atmosphere created by his severe presence at the head of the table and the unbelievably rude and dismissive way he spoke to his wife. He sat there and told us a string of very amusing anecdotes, impeccably delivered, but it was hardly a convivial occasion. Later I worked with his son, Matthew, at Nottingham and was made aware in several late night sessions where he poured his heart out that this was a seriously disturbed young man. On the other hand, my great friend Jean Holness, who understudied in a West End play with Sir Alec, has nothing but praise for his generosity. On learning that she, an insignificant member of the company, was currently mourning the death of her beloved dog, he left in her dressing room, complete with basket and other accoutrements, a magnificent black Persian cat, whom she immediately named Guinness, both because of her colour and her provenance. Guinness lived to be nearly twenty and was a very aristocratic and lordly being but she never liked me, or anyone besides Jean, and I never took to her. I used to feel very uncomfortable when she sat watching me fixedly, tail gently waving. I came to realise she was as enigmatic and complicated a being as her generous donor.

FOREIGN TOURS

Some actors will accept quite inferior parts in order to get in a tour abroad provided that the play itself and the director are reputable and the places to be seen interesting or even exciting. Georgine Anderson, the dear friend with whom I shared a flat in London for many years, frankly enjoyed seeing the world and was a valuable enough actress to ensure that her roles also were interesting. When she first left RADA she went off on impulse to work in Australia for four years, following it up with a year in Belfast before she took her first job in England at Colchester Rep, which was where I met her. My first job , and I found her a fascinating person besides being, to this day, one of my favourite actresses. Soon after we met again in London she was on an extended tour of the states with the RSC and not long after we moved in together she took off for a year to the Donovan Maule Repertory Theatre in Nairobi. I must relate, as they say, an amusing incident that occurred while she was there. The company had decided on doing a production of Agatha Christie's "Ten Little Niggers". This title had just begun to trouble the minds of people in the more aware sixties, before P.C. had finally been invented. The general consensus at the time was to call it "Ten Little Indians", though I remain baffled as to why this was thought less offensive. In those days, in Africa, the natives of the country recognised themselves as blacks and were not so conversant with American terminology as they are today. Consequently when the Director decided to consult a black stage-hand on the vexed question and tentatively mentioned the original title of the play, the man was puzzled. Then enlightenment dawned and he saw the source of the director's embarrassment. "Oh yes", he giggled. "You mean Ladies' Niggers!"

But I digress, as I believe they do say. I myself have not worked a great deal abroad. Partly, in the sixties, because I had the great opportunity of working over several years at the Royal Court Theatre which, as it concentrated largely on the work of new authors or unjustly neglected old plays, was just as appealing a proposition as a foreign tour, although quite ludicrously underpaid in comparison. In the seventies I had my children and did not wish to go far a field.

But the Court did give me the opportunity of a four day visit to Zurich with "Sergeant Musgrave's Dance" by John Arden and a three week tour of certain Iron Curtain countries with Edward Bond's "Narrow Road to the Deep North".

The excursion to Zurich took place in the summer months and the weather was glorious. The heat did not affect me so badly in those days, and the town sparkling around the great waters of the Zurich-See delighted us all. These were the swinging sixties and we were conscious of coming from a town that swung far in the lead of others at that time. It seems fashionable to decry the sixties now but it was certainly the best and happiest time of my life work-wise, and I cannot forget that after the earnest determination of the war years and the austerities and lingering outworn taboos of the fifties, the sense of release and ebullience of the sixties, plus the continuing pride of being British under the glittering mantle of the Beatles, was a heady mix. Perhaps we felt this more in the performing arts, untroubled by politics and working up to shaking off the ridiculous shackles of the censor who were a set of retired army gentlemen with very rigid and outmoded ideas of what constituted either blasphemy or bad-taste. They could not discern the difference between genuine thoughtful and committed plays which reflected the manners and language of ordinary people at that time and the sort of easy vulgarity and innuendo which I'm afraid the Carry-On series was often guilty of. The old soldiers were completely out of date. At the Royal Court we evaded their stifling embrace by putting on Sunday performances to so-called Club Members, where all was permissible – an inappropriate use of the Lord's Day I feel - and by reading out at rehearsal to great mirth their lists of words and phrases verboten which read like a smutty poem. A great case in point occurred for my character Annie in "Sergeant Musgrave". She was a warm and welcoming young woman working at the inn who accommodated the passing soldiery. The line was "Big strong Annie, open your arms and let them all in." This was too strong for the censor and in their elderly wisdom they directed that it should be, "Big strong Annie, open your arms and let them all come!" They were naïve as well.

Hey, this digression is becoming a way of life. You left me in, or on, the Zurich-See and I did indeed manage to get out on the lake rowed by Kenneth Cranham who had acquired a naval cap and the title of Midshipman Cranham in the company. I won't go in to the reasons why! You don't actually have much leisure time on these lightning theatrical visits as there is the question of setting up, lighting and rehearsing cues with an unknown, non-English speaking crew. Fortunately for us, if not for the production, there had been a slight hitch and our scenery had not arrived so we had time for disporting ourselves in the sun. It didn't arrive, in point of fact, until nearly the last minute and I was greatly impressed by the Swiss-German crew who erected the set with a speed and efficiency that would have set our stage-hands at home complaining to their union. Our assistant director sat beside their lighting designer and gave him his cues during the performance. A powerful achievement all round by the Swiss which made you perhaps not quite so proud to be British.

The behaviour of the company after the show was possibly also a little sub-standard. There was the usual generous dinner given for us and speeches of thanks after which some of the younger members of the company took some of the remaining bottles of wine off the tables and proceeded to the shores of the lake to continue festivities. We may have been rather loud but there was no vandalism, fighting or other disruption such as might have made us unwelcome today. My most abiding memory of that night is of Roger Booth, an actor who was an ex-army man who gave the most perfect solitary display of marching and counter-marching on a sort of jetty that jutted out into the water, accompanying himself with a faithful rendering of a military band, and who ended by solemnly walking off the end of the jetty into the lake, still at attention as it were.

Reprehensible, but we were predominately a young company of mavericks whose talents seemed to justify their wildness: such as Jack Shepherd, Ken Cranham, Denis Waterman and the brilliant but eccentric young Victor Henry who had a James Dean like death-wish but tragically only managed to have the sort of accident that rendered him a virtual vegetable for the rest of his life.

These then were among the company who, in 1969, were invited to go on a British Council Tour to communist parts, starting with a visit to Belgrade, relatively un-scary under Tito's rule, where "Saved", the other Edward Bond play we took, was to perform at a festival where it had won an award then, after an extraordinary diversion to Venice for the Biennale, on to Prague and then to Lublin and Warsaw in Poland. We had a couple of solemn visits from the Foreign Office who didn't quite trust our maverick members not to get into trouble with the authorities. British Council representatives would be responsible for us in each town or city and we were to be careful of our currency and to sell nothing. We would almost certainly be asked for blue jeans, which were very highly prized it appeared. We were to behave at all times as worthy ambassadors of our country. This was all very well, but as the rather working class and politically suspect Royal Court Theatre, we didn't get to play in the first-class theatres, as the RSC did. We were relegated to the equivalent of fringe or avant-garde establishments. Edward Bond, the author was to travel with us. He had, and has, a greater reputation abroad than in England and had already won awards, such as the one in Belgrade.

My dear friend, Nigel Hawthorne, later to be my son's godfather, and myself had time off in Belgrade as only "Saved" was playing there and I was very grateful to Nigel and to Edward who accompanied us whenever he was free, for guiding my sight-seeing during the very short times we had available during the whole tour. This included not only buildings, but the people. Nigel was very good at finding interesting people to talk to. I was a very ignorant person and wouldn't have known where to start. I had no idea, for instance, of the political situation in Jugoslavia and was astonished at the reception where we seemed exclusively to eat red or yellow peppers as kebabs, to be instructed by several earnest young men as to the superiority of the Serbs and the treachery of the Croats. I didn't even know that they lived there. I enjoyed our three days there and saw quite a few things including the Danube which disappointingly was not blue at all.

Our arrival in Venice was one of the magic moments of my life. It was approaching sunset as we entered by boat along the Grand Canal and I felt quite light headed and unreal a we disembarked at one of the crumbling awesome palaces and were given drinks at a reception where I found myself talking to Chaliapin's grand-daughter or great grand-daughter, can't remember which. Can't remember much about that evening as we hadn't eaten much all day and after changing into a sort of cat suit with wide flowing legs and, bizarrely an auburn wig, which we rather went in for in those days, I ran or rather floated along the streets of Venice feeling totally euphoric and like something out of "La Dolce Vita". A superb seafood supper soon put me right!

Being second class citizens we did not appear at the beautiful Fenice Theatre but at a place called the Palazzo Grassi which had a sort of corrugated roof upon which the rather frequent rain of Venice thundered the following night. However, this did not matter much as the Italians chatter during performances anyway. This does not appear to affect their enjoyment however and the reception at the end was a bit overwhelming for us Brits. In typical continental fashion they continued to applaud enthusiastically far beyond the call of duty and we didn't quite know where to put ourselves. I was busy accepting numerous bouquets and baskets of flowers and finally had to step forward and render hearty thanks and assure them that, as we were moving on soon, the flowers would find their way to the hopitale.

Only "Narrow Road" was playing in Venice so I was rather tired and did not accompany Nigel and Edward to one of the islands the next day to find Diaghilev's grave and place a rose on it, but this was when Edward first uttered his much-repeated phrase, "Nigel is Intrepid". He was certainly indefatigable.

After the luxury merchandise in the shops in Venice it was quite a cultural shock to arrive in Prague and experience the universal poverty of just about everything, particularly as it is a city with a comparable history and architectural treasures. But everything was so dirty and in poor repair. I have been back there for a television show in the nineties and only then did I see the gold roofs and the lovely buildings painted in yellow and pink and green. In 1969 they must have been covered in grime, and everywhere was drab, though nothing can quite obscure the beautiful lines of the Cathedral and Charles Bridge. The hotel could not produce any milk at breakfast time, nor butter for our bread – just a little jam. Our British Council hostess apologised for not entertaining us until the second half of our week's stay. "If I wait until after Wednesday," she said "We'll get the lorry from East Germany with some fresh lettuce."

We had to stay all together in a barrack-like motel place on the outskirts of the city and were warned not to venture out alone or at all after dark, except in the transport provided us. As we heard intermittent firing from some range nearby, we didn't feel inclined to. The one year anniversary of the Wenceslas Square riots fell during our week and we also knew that somewhere in the city the trial of Dubcek was taking place. "Saved" and "Narrow Road" were alternating here so on our nights off we were able to go to the opera. I saw "Jenufa" by Janacek with very heavy Germanic scenery which was very old fashioned by our standards but music and singing were splendid. We also saw a very patriotic piece called "Libusce" by Smetana, I think. I was entranced by a very large static soprano with more vibrato than you could shake a baton at. Her name was Maria Podfalova and I thought it very apt: she was very wobbly whenever she moved. But the line of Czech kings stretching back to the mists of time (rather reminiscent of Macbeth) went down very well with the indigenous population. And so, indeed, did our play. "Narrow Road" is a play about tyrants and oppression and was received with enthusiasm and intelligence. Our director told us that the simultaneous translation was quite brilliant and we could tell because we got our laughs even quicker on cue than at the Court. Several youths managed to contact us during the daytime and were eager to discuss the play and their own rebellious feelings with us. Nigel even managed to get invited to someone's home. But on the whole we found that the young people did not speak English. Russian was their second language. The older people spoke German of course, and as Edward's Austrian girl friend, Elizabeth, later his wife, had joined us during a four hour flight hiatus in Vienna she was able to provide us with an interpreter.

And so on to Poland. Our planes were getting more and more elderly and one of them was alleged by the boys to have come out of a cereal packet. They swore they had seen "cut along the dotted line" on the side. Ken Cranham suggested we should all put our feet through the floor and help pedal it off the runway.

Lublin was a town that time seemed to have forgotten. The last English company to go there was supposed to be in the 16th Century. The people were fascinated by us and, as these were the days of long hair for us, our young Irish ASM found one curious spectator feeling his chest to see if he were a girl or not: his hair was very curly. The same lack of variety of food as in Prague obtained in the hotel. We went to one small restaurant rather like a café where people got up and danced in a manner reminiscent of the forties in wartime England. They did not appear to be very au fait with the news and we were assured that the Russians had sent tanks into Prague the previous year because they were in danger of being over-run by the Germans. There being no simultaneous translation the play was received in dead silence, but it was a silence of extreme concentration and the applause at the end was overwhelming.

Edward insisted that Nigel and I accompany him to the concentration camp Majdanek which was nearby. Here the silence had quite another quality and the stark buildings with their ovens and cells were achingly empty except for one cell filled to the roof with the distinctive Jewish caps and others with just the marks of fingernails on the ceiling. This was even more affecting than the Jewish cemetery in Prague which was just a mass of tombstones all huddled together with hardly an inch of space between.

Our final destination was Warsaw where we were to perform in the "Palace of Culture", a new building looking like a layered wedding cake. Here we rubbed shoulders with embassy staff as well as British Council and I met with an ambassador who much admired our Queen because she had always "done her homework" and someone from Athens who, when I mentioned that my partner came from Guiseley in Yorkshire instantly said triumphantly "Harry Ramsden's!" I saw a production of St Joan on my night off and was driven there and back in an embassy car in which my host looked back and said "That's my tail. He's the one who always follows me. You'd miss them if they weren't there."

The main square in Warsaw had been completely destroyed by the Germans towards the end of the war whilst Stalin sat outside and let them do it as he waited to move in and take over. The entire space had been lovingly rebuilt from photographs to be absolutely identical, including the house which the Golem haunted. I wonder if he ever came back to it.

The weather became icy in Warsaw, as we were now into October and I arrived back home with Bronchitis. My partner had grown worried because he hadn't received any letters since Venice. They all arrived in a bunch after I got home. I got his alright though, and at the hotel Metropole Warsaw I received his proposal of marriage. Fortunately he was inclined to be dyslexic and asked if we should get "maride". I always felt this wasn't binding. However I went to the one official shop where you could buy things to take out of the country and bought him a beer stein as an engagement present. No less than three of us got married almost immediately after our return. It had been that sort of a trip.

My wedding day was October 25th. I still had quite a bad cough at the time.

CANADIAN ADVENTURE

My only other venture into working outside these shores took place in 1970 and I think of it as "The Great Canadian Adventure". The omens that year all seemed to point firmly towards Canada. First of all I was in a production of Caesar and Cleopatra by G.B.S. at the Sybil Thorndike Theatre Leatherhead, where the eponymous roles were played by Canadians Tobi Robbins (she was a woman) and William Hutt who was a leading light at the Festival Theatre Stratford Ontario and had just arrived in England for a little change of scene. From him I learned a great deal about the company over in Stratford who were obviously very close to his heart, not least the surprising fact that there were several escapees from our Young Vic Theatre in the fifties, a company which I had seen and admired in a couple of memorable plays at that time, not least Goldoni's "A Servant of Two Masters". I am an especial fan of Goldoni and it had stuck in my mind. These ex-Brits had become really assimilated over in Canada it appeared, had married Canadians and had introduced a cricket team against much initial indifference. Bill Hutt was a very good actor and his stories of the Festival Theatre inspired me with great enthusiasm.

Not long after this I did an episode of "Softly, Softly", which I greatly enjoyed as I was the murderer – with an axe! My partner in the episode was played by Douglas Rains, also a visitor from Stratford Ontario. He too was an enthusiast and urged me to accept without delay the offer my agent received for me at this time.

Irene Worth had been a frequent visitor to the Royal Court Theatre when I was playing there and had come round on several occasions with very generous praise for my performances and had even sent flowers on first nights. She had appeared in the very first season at Stratford in 1953 and was a great patron of the theatre to which she returned to perform from time to time. She had now been asked to play Hedda Gabler in the 1970 season and she wanted me to with her as Mrs Elsvsted. They pretty well bowed to her will over there and she had also suggested Gordon Jackson as Tesman and Peter Gill as our director. The rest of the casting she graciously left up to the Canadians! Peter was a very old friend of mine and I had also worked with Gordon at the Court so I looked all set for a very good time. I was only to appear in this one play in the repertoire and so would have plenty of time to explore the country. The only snag was that I had just got married the previous October at the end of our Iron Curtain Countries tour. I did not really want to leave my husband for four or five months so early in our married life.

"No problem", said the Stratford Theatre. "Bring your husband along. We'll pay for his ticket."

"No problem whatsoever" said my husband, who at the time was a free-lance illustrator and graphic designer – but more importantly a keen fisherman. "I'll bring my rods along."

So, in April we flew off to Canada, happy in the knowledge that the warm weather would be just beginning. Stratford Ontario is about ninety miles form Toronto, which is not as far as it sounds given their wide, straight roads and powerful cars. It is a town that grew around the railway and the big Canadian trains came through at all times of the day and night on tracks that were unfenced and divided the town at a point between the theatre and our comfortable little basement flat home with an Italian family. We were possibly the wrong side of the tracks as all the important buildings were near the theatre site, but they were a very friendly family and we were very happy with them. The deep clanging noise the trains made in the night had a friendly sound and seemed to emphasise the vast size of the country we were now in. This impression was reinforced by the feeling that the sky was much farther away than at home and by the sound and fury of the thunderstorms that occurred at regular intervals. The weather pattern seemed to be that it was dry for ten days or so with the heat slowly increasing until it got to a pitch where we would have a thunderstorm, torrential rain and then clear skies again. This was handy because, unlike in changeable England, you always knew roughly when you would need rainwear or umbrella and could confidently ignore them the rest of the time. Mind you, although I started off walking into the theatre each day I soon found that the natives thought I was mad. Taxis were cheap, we were all well paid and nobody walked. And it was true that there was a notable absence of pedestrians all the time I was there. We soon became accustomed to telephoning for a pizza or to the dry cleaners, or wherever. That sort of delivery service and indeed that sort of food hadn't really hit us back in England at that time. Kentucky Fried Chicken was also a brand new concept to us.

We soon discovered the importance of having a telephone in our flat and my husband got in touch with the amazing Bell Telephone Company for whom I have nothing but the greatest praise and admiration. We could have a telephone straight away they said and, had we had one before? Surprised my husband said,

"Well, of course, we had one in London."

"Fine", they said, "there will be no installation charge." Only later did we discover that you only pay the very first time you have a telephone with the Bell Company, and secondly that there is a small town quite near Stratford called London. There's one called Paris just down the road.

Local calls with the company were all free and trunk calls, even to remote towns in the UK were put through with a speed and efficiency to which we were quite unaccustomed. When we left Canada we notified Bell and asked for our last bill as we were returning to England.

"Don't worry", they said. "We'll find you and bill you wherever you are." They did too.

Early on we bought a cheap barbecue, rather like an upturned dustbin on legs and my husband, who is a very good cook, soon abandoned the cooker in our flat and put everything on the barbecue outside – even the Sunday roast joint.

Booze however was a different ball game. Bottled beer, which was divided into beer and ale, (I never quite knew the difference) could be delivered by the crate from the Brewers Retail. But all other alcohol, known as Liquor, could only be obtained from the one official Liquor Store, a place where the Liquor was all kept behind bars and you filled in a chit for what you wanted, took it to the man at the desk who took your money, and then unlocked the cage and produced your bottle. Ontario was very much a Scottish Presbyterian settled province and the liquor laws were strict. You could not drink outside, not even in your own garden. You could not drink on Sunday. There were places you could go to have a drink as unlike a pub as possible. There you had to be seated and waited on and the beer came in jugs. One of these places had two entrances: one with ladies over it and one with gentlemen. These were no longer in use as such and you all joined up inside anyway.

At the theatre there was a special system. When you collected your salary each week you could buy strips of tickets, different colours for ale / beer and for Liquor. These could be exchanged for the appropriate beverage at the theatre bar, which was in a vast room with two full-size pool tables in the centre and seating round the outside. Here you did not have to be waited on or sit down but I think it was all to do with the fact that no money actually changed hands.

This bar was in the second theatre in the town. A proscenium arch theatre, predictably called the A-von, where the more modern plays of the season were put on. The Festival Theatre itself was an impressive and large building. It had started life in 1953 as a tent for the first few seasons and when they came to build the theatre they had kept the shape of a marquee with a central flagpole and festive awnings. There was a great deal of ceremony attached to the opening of the season and they had trumpeters dressed as heralds on the balconies to mark the occasion. It was an impressive auditorium consisting of a thrust stage with an Elizabethan-type Upper Stage, or balcony at the back, and an entrance either side of this with steps down. The stage was raised so that there were three steps up from the audience, and to the left and right and under the seating were sloping tunnels so that entrances could also be made from the front of the stage. This was an obvious advantage for Shakespeare and other period dramas but it was a little tricky for us with Hedda Gabler originally designed for a proscenium arch theatre. It meant that we had to find reasons during quite intimate dialogue scenes for crossing to the other side of the stage in order to give that side of the house a favourable glimpse of our profiles. A great deal of the play has two-handed scenes where people are quite naturally sitting and chatting.

Fortunately Hedda is restive and Thea Elvsted nervous, so fairly credible reasons for movement were found. The acoustics were very good but we did have some complaints that our English accents were hard to understand!

The stage had originally been designed by Tyrone Guthrie, the director, and Tanya Moseiwich, the designer, and they had gone on to build a similar one in the United States. Tanya Moseiwich came back to design the production of Cymbeline for the 1970 season and her use of the stage and her set were an object lesson in how effective such a theatre could be. Her costumes were bold and colourful and impressed my husband forever, particularly as this was the first Shakespeare play he had ever seen performed.

There was an army of wardrobe men and women, all mostly imported from the Old Vic Theatre in London it appeared. Familiar London accents predominated. Even shoes and boots were made in the theatre at enormous cost. The costume budgets were very generous, as were their salaries. We had brought Deidre Clancy, my favourite designer from the Royal Court, with us and she was able to afford very superior materials for Hedda. We had many regular costume fittings scheduled in our daily rehearsals, not snatched after hours or between scenes as they usually were at home. Consequently our costumes were superb and I would have loved to bring mine home with me. I should have loved to be able to buy one of Deidre's designs for me but these were sold for large sums to Canadian theatre-lovers and reverently framed by them.

Rehearsal time was also very generous and we had a chance to study the play intimately in its brand new adaptation by Christopher Hampton who also came over from London for some rehearsals and for the opening. Unfortunately, Irene, having chosen Peter Gill specially to direct did not always see eye to eye with him. She was a little old fashioned in her approach and Peter is very modern and dynamic. He is a very intelligent man and Irene, by contrast was an "intellectual" in inverted commas. She was a great friend of Sir Kenneth Clark and prided herself on her intellectual understanding. I know she had read a lot and held discussions with the great minds of her day but she didn't always seem to grasp the basic honesty and directness of Peter's approach to the play and I found myself acting as a sort of interpreter of ideas to her because she had enlisted my help in learning her lines and we went over our scenes quite a lot. I found it an uncomfortable position between my loyalty to Peter and my very real admiration for Irene. What I was never brave enough to tell her was that when she acted out of instinct she had the most amazing dynamic impact that knocked you breathless at times, but when she intellectualised it just didn't ring quite true.

Of course she was far too old for the role but, such a beautiful and charismatic woman still, that it hardly mattered. Because of Irene's age the character of Aunt Julie was being played by an American actress called Ann Ives, who had had her first part in 1906. She was unashamedly of her era and naturally would have preferred a proscenium arch theatre but she was just right for the conventional Aunt Julie and she simply ignored anything she felt was too much like method acting. She was very spry for her age and had a sweet nature and a great sense of humour. We shared a dressing room and corresponded for a short while after I came home.

Our Judge Brack was an actor called Donald Davies who was also playing Shylock that season. Lovborg was played by a temperamental, slightly awkward but basically generous natured actor called Leo Ciceri. I was very sad to hear after I had left Canada that he was killed in a car crash later in the season. Gordon Jackson, of course, was perfect casting for the fussy, precise Tesman, Hedda's husband. Gordon himself agonises every step of the way over his work and if you look at his script you can hardly see the lines for all the notes he has written to himself. Tesman to the life! Yet he is a superb instinctive actor and rarely puts a foot wrong. The cast was completed by Berthe the maid, played by a seasoned Canadian actress, wife of Mervyn Blake, one of the aforementioned English actors from the Young Vic company who was well established and contented over there both on stage and on the cricket pitch.

The play opened to great acclaim and on the first night we were presented after the performance to the Governor General, His Excellency the Right Hon Roland Michener. We stood in line, Irene at the head and I was next to her. To my horror she not only sank into the deepest and most graceful curtsey I have ever seen but then, turning and putting her arm around me she said in deep tones. "And this is our beloved Gillian Martell." I was so flustered I don't know whether I bowed, bobbed, or just shook hands muttering charmed, or enchantée, or something equally fatuous. I was extremely gratified to receive a very favourable personal review from Clive Barnes, the dreaded New York critic in his American paper. I had had to join American Equity as Canada didn't at that time have a separate union and when I left the country I applied for Temporary Withdrawal. This withdrawal has now become very permanent!

Once we opened we had our days free and quite a lot of free evenings. We were able to see all the other plays in the repertoire, several of them with other British actors heading the casts and one amazing one-off one man show given by Marcel Marceau. He very generously gave all the actors and stage staff a whole morning where he talked to us, answered questions and demonstrated his art. Unforgettable! My husband was able to get his fishing and had found a friend in the town who seemed to enjoy nothing better than to drive us around to various rivers and other beauty spots and also for a swim in Lake Huron which at that time was less polluted than some of the other lakes. Lake Erie being notably quite dead, so they said. Irene too had a great many friends in the town and insisted on including me and my husband in many of her invitations so we got to see some interesting private homes. If she wanted to take us sight seeing she would ruthlessly commandeer any other free actor who had a car and generously allow them to chauffeur us to wherever she wanted to go. Our trips were mostly confined to Ontario, we didn't get over to the west or indeed to the French side but we did get as far as Niagara which is extremely impressive if you turn your back on all the honeymoon motels and neon signs and do not raise your eyes towards the dark Satanic Mills of Buffalo on the American side.

We decided to cash in our return air fares and return home by sea. We had a choice of sailing from the St Lawrence and seeing something of Quebec province or from New York. In the end the choice was made for us by Dick Cuyler, an American University Drama Teacher who had had a year's sabbatical, some of which he had spent with us at the Royal Court, studying our methods – with a small M. He and his wife wanted to come up to the last night of Hedda and then drive us back to stay a week with them at Saratoga Springs before driving us to New York to catch the sailing of the "France" on the glamorous French Line. This gave us the opportunity to see something of the States on our car journey. We then spent a wonderful week in Saratoga Springs, which I thought of as an American version of Cheltenham as it was a Spa, had a Music Festival and a nationally important race track. We were lucky enough to be there during a race week and were taken to have a breakfast of waffles and maple syrup at the track. I took several photographs of the races but when they came out there was not a horse in sight – they were all too quick for me.

By now it was late August and my chief impression of New York was of a humidity that was like being wrapped in warm flannels. But all the long straight streets in New York go down to the river so we got an impressive vista as we stood at the rail sailing down to wave goodbye at last to the Statue of Liberty and then luxuriate in our five-day cruise home. Being a French ship, although you had to pay for spirits, there was a free bottle of red and one of white on the table at every meal. The South African couple we shared a table with did not drink so my husband was able to indulge himself freely and to avail himself of what he told me was a good cure for a hangover to which he was also indebted to the French – onion soup for breakfast!

I was not able to help him out much with either soup or wine because I was then in the early stages of pregnancy.

FISHING VIGNETTE

When I hear the sound of waves advancing and retreating rhythmically over pebbles I am back in my bedroom in the house at Southwold. A house of so many happy memories for countless numbers of my friends and relations, who holidayed there, got engaged there, were married and / or honeymooned there. I am back in my bedroom particularly because it is at night that the sound is so clear and so soothing.

The bedroom window is open so that I can smell the sea as well as hear it. The curtains with their brown and green sampans on a white ground are periodically lit by the four flashes from the lighthouse which is behind our house but lights the sea with a gentle glow. The vivid 'savannah' green I painted the walls shines more softly in this friendly light. The door to the tiny cupboard-like room opening off mine which I always thought of as a 'powder-closet' and used to have a small dressing table in, now contains a cot where our son of a few months is sleeping. My husband is out, fishing on the end of the pier – not the smart longer pier which they have recently built there, but the old short pier, never fully restored from war and storms and of interest only to fishermen. I am drowsily content.

Presently I hear the sound of my husband's Wellingtons squelching past the window and then the distant sound of the front door – never locked in Southwold in those days. In a few minutes the smell of the sea and of fish comes strongly into the room as my husband, minus Wellingtons but still in his strong smelling old Barbour, comes excitedly into the room. I gather I must instantly accompany him downstairs to view the catch. Grumbling softly, so as not to wake our son, I do so, but when we reach the kitchen my complaints die away and I am suddenly wide awake. Lying across the sink and across two draining boards either side is the largest cod I have ever see, deceased but regrettably still twitching slightly as I gaze. The head is disproportionately huge. The colour still sea-water bright. Much larger cod are of course caught out at sea in the deep water, but from the beach, or even the truncated pier, no! This is a marvellous prize and I sense my husband cannot wait for daylight and the time when he can go to the pub with his trophy to amaze his friends among the local fishermen. He had stayed alone on the pier after others had departed and this was his reward. I congratulate him suitably and sincerely. He is going to have a wonderful day tomorrow.

I leave him to the unpleasant business of gutting his monster and ascend the stairs to try to re-capture the tranquillity of my nocturnal waves, but fear I have been too sharply reminded of the more savage aspects of the ocean – or of man?.

ROSE

As an actress I am not a very West End person. My soul shrinks from the idea of a too-long run. I enjoy above everything being part of a company, but not the sort that you find in London where the members are living scattered over a wide metropolis with their own pursuits and, probably, their own families. The camaraderie of the theatre may obtain in the evenings with a little extra on Matinee days but it is far removed from the bonds created in a repertory company, where people live closely together with the same aims and ideas and with a stimulating variety of plays to concentrate on. You get to know each other's habits and capabilities and this enriches performance but you can still be startled out of complacency by a piece of 'interesting' casting or the demands of a provocatively inspiring play. Such leisure time as there is, is usually spent together but familiarity mostly breeds loyalty and respect, rather than contempt.

Even at the Royal Court Theatre where I spent a lot of time, the same feeling is there, with the added bonus that you are often doing completely new plays for the very first time and you get to work closely with the authors as well. Added to which the company consists generally of comparatively 'unknown' non-starry actors and such giants of the theatre as do frequently join the company do so as part of a team and though respected for their achievements are not accorded any particular status within the company.

It is ironic then, that one of the most fulfilling times of my life took place in the West End theatre in 1980. For this there were several reasons.: the play itself "Rose", written by Andrew Davies, only then just embarking on his successful TV career as adaptor of the classics. The director, Alan Dosser, had been in the company at Nottingham Playhouse, chiefly remembered by me for his contempt for pantomimes. He had been one of the villagers in "Jack and the Beanstalk" and was rather apt to skip some of their appearances and remain in his dressing room saying he had better things to do and would not be missed. Even then he was working towards a career as a director and when he came to cast "Rose" he drew on his acquaintance with good, solid actors rather than TV stars possibly better known to the public. He had his "star" to attract the punters, Glenda Jackson, but brilliant as she undoubtedly is on stage Glenda might almost be termed an anti-star. True to her socialist principles she has refused all honours and resolutely eschewed any form of glamour in dress, makeup or leisure activities. She is the same girl from Liverpool as she was when we were at RADA together in the fifties with the addition of a quiet no-fuss confidence which results from the knowledge of good work well-done.

The rest of the cast were of the same complexion – knowing what they were capable of, used to working hard as a team but above all, as was to emerge, sharing the same lively sense of humour.

There was Jean Heywood, known at that time for her sensitive portrait of the Mother in "When the Boat Comes in", warm, funny, generous and proudly Geordie and, in my opinion, one of our greatest actresses. Nobody can move me to tears as Jean can, and has done since in many TV performances, not least because the laughter is never far away.

There was David Daker, from Coventry, where incidentally the play was set – a man with hidden depths, quiet charm and consummate skill.

Tom Georgeson, also from Liverpool like Glenda, fresh from triumph in Alan Bleasdale's "Black Stuff", but like the rest of us with a solid body of good theatre work behind him. Dear Tom! He always wore red on Saturdays in support of his Liverpool team and I would indulge him by doing the same, as he lived near me at Teddington and used to chauffeur me to the theatre and back.

Diana Davies from Manchester: full of warm bubbling humour and Northern forthrightness. She alone had no rep experience but had started out life as an extra in "A Family at War", been noticed, given a small speaking part and graduated inevitably to "Corrie" where she made her mark by behaving as her own down-to-earth self. Di acted as she breathed, no need for training or rep. in her case. She was true all through and not proud. After "Rose" she crossed the Pennines and settled comfortably in "Emmerdale Farm". She belonged in the North – she exemplified all its best characteristics. She, of course, was a visitor in London and living in digs, but she never lacked invitations to our homes for the weekend. She had that essential gift in a visitor, completely at ease with herself and accepting you as she expected to be accepted. She could help in practical ways about the house, or with the children whilst intuitively never upsetting the routine or putting anything in the wrong place. A sort of domestic chameleon she was absorbed into and enriched any background. And she's quite unaware of how priceless she is.

Last but not least my dear Stephanie Cole, funny, sensitive, talented artistic, hard working – dedicated even – completely sincere and, at this time, unconfident having nearly given up the business in despair. All the rest of the cast had long duologue scenes with Glenda, as her Mother, her husband, her lover and her best friend, but Steff and I came as a package, good old Battcock and Cockshott. We were Glenda's fellow teachers, featuring her in a work relationship, Steff as the severe and unsympathetic Headmistress, me as the incompetent but earnest Junior Mistress with problems. Our scenes were more overtly comic and less moving than the rest of the play as was natural from our less intimate relationship with the protagonist. But we had one scene in the second half which Steff and I labelled "The Atrocity Scene", with Steff furious and me tearful over vandalism in the classroom. "Chopped up Goldfish and excrement all over the walls", fumed Steff and one tired night well into the run it became "Chopped up excrement and goldfish all over the walls." Those goldfish became the symbols of everything vile in our society.

The play was put on by Colin Brough and his new "Lupton Theatre Company". He and his wife, Helen, a nurse, were charming people very eager and interested in this new experience of producing. We saw rather more of them than one generally does of a producer and they treated us all as friends. The Duke of York's theatre had just been taken over and completely refurbished by Capital Radio so even the building felt new and exciting, the dressing rooms unusually clean and comfortable and Capital Radio anxious to respond to any suggested improvements. Perhaps it was this unusual luxury and concern surrounding us, not least from our wonderful Company Manager, Christine Roberts, who was a sort of Mother-cum-Counsellor to us all, bringing us gossip of who was in the audience and what they said and did, which made us all decide that we wanted to share our leisure activities as well as our work. We were such a happy band of people and so much on the same wavelength particularly when you add into the mix our stage management team: severe but heart of gold Margaret attempting to control us all; teasable Peter and bubbly Sheila her assistants, warm motherly but lively Bobby our wardrobe mistress and special mention – Peggy Shields from South Shields, understudying Jean and keeping us in fits with her vagueness and inconsequential remarks. Even the Lighting Designer was good old Andy Phillips from the Royal Court, set designer John Gunter whom I had first met in Coventry and knew well and Lindy Hemmings our costume designer who was new but who satisfactorily passed the test of a tactful attitude towards my dress size.

The play was unusually organised, as I've said, into a series of long scenes of individuals with Glenda (Steff and I being one) and therefore all of us, except poor Glenda, having ample time off for chat and gossip and even as the run went on a Bridge four in the second half with people taking over a hand as somebody was called away. Pegs, the understudy, was useful here as she was obviously free all the time and her vagueness and her eccentric bidding added greatly to the enjoyment. Activities began to develop as the very successful run continued – we had long queues for returns every night and were booked solid for the whole six months. It started with birthdays – some of us had them during the run, others didn't and were allocated official birthdays. All names were put into a hat and we had to make a large card for our particular designate with cut-out pictures and verbal comments relevant to either the actor or their character in the play. These were very ingenious and successful. Then Colin's wife, Helen, announced her pregnancy and we all embroidered a set of nappies with our initials for her. (I must admit Steff did mine for me as she is a notable needlewoman and embroideress and I cannot sew a note.) Steff was elected our Social Secretary and organised various outings for us, such as a visit to a newly opened gay club nearby which occasioned much hilarity. We had various parties on Sundays – at Jean's lovely house, Chapel Pines, whose name gives you a great clue to its beauty. She had a wonderful garden, tended by her husband, Roland. They grew two different varieties of peas and as they ripened Jean would bring the pods into the dressing room at night for us to munch the peas raw and sweet. Christine Roberts too, gave a big party as company manager for everyone connected with the show at her large country estate. We all took our children to that one and one of Glenda's numerous sisters also appeared from Liverpool. Or were there two of them? They all look like her anyway.

I had scored quite a success with my first night gifts. I had photocopied and framed various Victorian saucy postcards from a book I had, and stuck a suitable quote from the play on each. They went down well and started a fashion for similar achievements. There were various in-jokes connected with the play which occasioned some witty drawings and histories which we pinned on our doors. The comment in the Press about Jean as Glenda's mother being like a parrot sitting on her shoulder was an obvious source for these. Steff and Di had chosen, for some reason I have forgotten, to view each other as race horses and many illustrations and bulletins from the stables appeared. We all seemed to stimulate each other to heights of wit never achieved before or since and Steff decided to collect all these together into a little booklet as a souvenir along with comments overheard from the audience by Christine and her minions. The play was a must for visiting Americans that year and some of the distinctly northern expressions tended to baffle them. As in one fragment:

American man (to Englishman sitting in the circle) – Excuse me, could you tell me what this word "Kecks" means?

Englishman – Well, I would imagine trousers, wouldn't you?

Some time later: Englishman – "Shaft", do you understand that?

A New Zealander was heard to say – It's all very well, but I don't know how it'll go down back home.

And an elderly man – Two things have shocked me, not having been to the theatre for years: the price of the seats and the language. But I didn't feel insulted. You know, you find them and you feel them and you .... Forget them. This in reference to Di's line concerning her attitude to men. "Find 'em, feel 'em, fuck 'em and forget 'em."

And in the bar:

American Lady to barmaid – Excuse me, but is Glenda Jackson bisexual?

Barmaid (shocked) – I really don't know.

American Lady – Well, would you find out and if she is, I'm giving a party in Florida on Saturday night and I'd love her to come. And you can come with her!

Everybody came to the show: Rock Hudson, Charlton Heston, during Wimbledon week Rosie Casals and Martina Navratilova. Set in Coventry as the play was, there was much talk of cars. Tom's character seducing Glenda's with the offer of sex in his Maxi, which she accepted, causing her later to say in one of her chats to the audience "Oh, Michael Edwardes, you don't advertise those cars the right way at all!" This brought Michael Edwardes himself along to see what all the fuss was about! It is a pleasant feeling being in an unequivocally acknowledged success and we all loved the play anyway. It made for a magic six months and left the four of us, Jean, Steff Di and myself, as lifelong better-than-friends.

We have all had our ups and downs since, illnesses bereavements as well as triumphs at work and families growing up at home. We have all supported each other in joy and sorrow and continue to do so. The achievements of one are felt and shared by all. The three of us were there in the studio when Steff had her "This is Your Life", disgracing herself when Michael Aspel appeared at the curtain call of her current play. She caught sight of him in the wings and, though the applause covered all sound, her lips were clearly seen to enunciate "Oh Fuck!" But it's a good life, all the same.

MOTHER'S LITTLE HELPERS

In the entertainment business it is essential to keep one's name preferably before the public but at least before the minds, and hopefully hearts, of agents and casting directors. One must constantly be either working or available. This presents a problem for the working mother whose mind and heart are, in most cases, heavily focused on her offspring.

In my case, when my first child was born my husband was still a freelance illustrator and graphic designer and compromises could be reached. From the start I wished to share as much of my child's early years as possible without giving rise to that dire phrase on casting directors' lips, "Oh no, she's given it up!" So I told my agent that the time had come for us to concentrate more on television where I could rack up short term engagements. (I didn't contemplate long-running soaps, and series lasting over several months of the year were thinner on the ground then than now.) In this way we could stall theatre directors by indicating the child's tender years but implying heavy involvement in television: mother caring, but actress still up and running. I always knew that I had to continue to work in order to remain the sort of person by whom I should wish my children to be brought up, and I had seen too many cases of women who had given up for several years and were frantically trying to get back to want to join their ranks.

When my second child was on the way my husband decided that it was time for him to get a more steady and reliable job and through the good offices of friends he applied for and got a job with Thames television as a scenic artist. This meant that he was travelling to Teddington every day from North London and after the trauma of my daughter's birth when I was in hospital for three months and my son had perforce to go to my parents in Bedford, we realised that it was essential we move to Teddington so that my husband could be more available in future.

So I left my beloved maisonette in Primrose Hill and moved south of the river to a three-storey house in Teddington just round the corner from the station which would help me to work in the future, but also very close to Bushey Park which was great for the children. My husband could, of course, walk to work and there were some very good pubs on the way back should I not require his attendance.

We could not afford a Nanny and did not need one as my work was sporadic, but we did need someone to be there whenever a job came up. And so I entered the world of Mother's Helps. These girls were usually anything between seventeen and twenty-two years old – I had to buy a serious amount of eighteenth and even twenty-first birthday presents during this time. Some of them had been in care and abruptly pushed out into the world at sixteen so that they were in need of a mother and a sense of family back-up as much as I needed them.

The first girl we had, who remained with us for some time and constantly came back to visit us afterwards, was called Lyn. She had a heart bursting with love for children and for us, an insatiable desire to be loved herself and a restless longing to express herself and achieve some half-understood goal in life which would make her feel like a worthwhile person. This feeling had been planted in her at school where endless vistas of careers and potential attainment had been paraded before her which, without the backing of family support and encouragement, not to mention financial assistance, she was unlikely to achieve. Her love of children led her to us and her involvement with our two was total. They loved her very much and my daughter's first complete sentence was uttered to me when I was changing her nappy and she smiled up at me saying "Lyn'll do it!" She was completely trustworthy and competent and I was able to do what jobs came up with a quiet mind. At the same time her half-comprehended ambitions prompted her to spend her money on a guitar and guitar lessons. She had a small but sweet singing voice and she was taking the only path to success obvious to her in the seventies.

Inevitably after she left us she became pregnant not once but three times, by different fathers and she would wheel them over in prams and pushchairs to see us. The system which she had left at sixteen was once again housing her and she was doing cleaning jobs for extras. The children were beautifully cared for and I hope she found her obvious maternal love fulfilling enough. Maybe one day she even found someone to love her as much as she wanted. I don't know. We lost touch when we left Teddington.

Our next employee, Anthea, was very different, except in so far as she too was fond of children but in her case without needing anything back from them. She was Asian and had a large family living in a neighbouring district. She stayed with us during the week and all her social life took place during the week-ends when she went back to her home. She had no desire to go out in the evenings during the week but preferred to stay in her own room with the television. Consequently I was free to join my husband at the pub or for a meal whenever I wanted to. Anthea was not exactly lazy but she was laid back. She was slow-moving but conscientious with her work, and when this was done she didn't move much. Everything had to be explained to her carefully and when she understood she would carry out commands to the letter. When she joined us we were in the middle of the drought in the summer of seventy-six and I asked her to save the children's bath water so that my husband could use it when he came home for the vegetable garden. When the drought broke and we had torrential rain Anthea still religiously saved the bath water. A routine was a routine to her and she wasn't going to be put off by any intellectualising. I liked her. She was very restful.

We had several girls after that for a short time while they decided what they were going to do with their lives but the one that stands out in memory, and will do forever more, was Sharon. I think she was one whom we got through "The Lady" magazine where, sandwiched among the highly qualified, high class nannies, you could at that time find a few "Mother's Helps" whose parents wanted them to find a respectable family to work for. Sharon must have been found this way because her parents lived somewhere distant like Kent and ran a village shop, which included a Post Office which rather tied them to the spot as the hours were rigid. They spoke to us on the phone though and were obviously loving and anxious parents.

Sharon was a very pleasant, quite eager girl who got on well with the children and seemed to be happy within the family circle. She came with us to my parent's holiday home in Southwold where there was a slight incident at the fireworks display on the common. She somehow got a spark in her eye which did become rather inflamed and required a great deal of sympathy and attention for her, which she appeared rather to enjoy. Soon after we returned to Teddington I got a T.V. job lasting two to three weeks. One night Sharon was stricken with stomach pains and we had to call the doctor. He examined her and questioned her and then took me aside to explain that he had not been able to make a proper examination because her stomach was so rigid and that he felt he had better take her into hospital for observation to be on the safe side. In a couple of days she was back and seemingly recovered, my job was finishing, and my husband had filled the breach. Sharon seemed happy again. Some time later I got the offer of a theatre job I didn't wish to refuse: a limited run at the Royal Court. This meant I would be away for rehearsals and than at night for the run of three weeks. Not impossible domestically and it would keep up my contact with the theatre. It was then that the nightmare began.

Someone, it appeared, was stalking Sharon. She received anonymous notes stuck with pieces of cut out newspaper print. My husband enlisted various friends at our local pub a hundred yards or so away, where he would call in regularly after work. He had stayed at home with Sharon for several nights and nothing had occurred, so he went back to his usual routine telling her to ring him there at the Railway Inn if there was any sort of incident. Almost immediately such an incident occurred. She rang the pub to say a window had been broken in our house and she was frightened. My husband ran down the road arriving in a couple of minutes and two of his friends went the other way down the alley from the station which approached our house from the other side. When they converged nobody had seen anyone, suspicious or otherwise. They remained on stand by for several nights during which time Sharon received more threatening messages. My husband had taken to keeping his cricket bat by the bed at night but I was not at all happy with the situation. We sent the children off for a week's holiday to stay with my parents in Bedford and Sharon accompanied them, both to help my mother and to get her out of the firing line as it were. A couple of nights later my husband wakened me abruptly from a from a deep sleep saying, "I knew it was her all along." When the sleep cleared from my brain he explained that he had searched Sharon's room and found the newspapers with the cut out pieces. We discussed the situation and alerted my parents by phone the next morning. It was decided that we should not say anything to her but ring her parents and explain what had occurred. They were devastated and wanted her home but were unable to leave their post office unattended. So my mother told Sharon that we thought she needed a rest at home after what she had been through. The children were happy in Bedford and Sharon took her ticket money and cheerfully went off to Kent. That was the last we saw of her. Looking back I think that that doctor had indicated that she was a possible hysteric and it was also obvious to us that she was not happy as soon as I went off to work.

Determined next time to make a better choice I actually interviewed and engaged a girl called Caroline from an advertisement in "The Lady". She had her N.N.E.B. qualification and I felt I was being responsible and clever. All the other girls I had chosen because I had felt some sort of rapport with and liking for them. I did not dislike Caroline but neither did I instinctively like her. This feeling proved to be mutual. She did not fit in with our family and from the first rather put my back up by her suspicious attitude. She was very jealous of her rights – her father was a trades union official it turned out. When I was not working life was very easy for the girls. They were all able to have a social life, more or less as they wanted and things had always worked well with a bit of give and take. Caroline wanted rules and our lives were not run according to rule. We parted with no regrets on either side.

By far the happiest five or six months we had were with the only older girl, Nancy Mazotta an Australian of Italian extraction well into her twenties. She wanted a job for the winter months to save money towards touring the continent in the summer when her Australian boy-friend would join her and then they would return to Oz together. By great good luck she was a hairdresser so we all had free hair-dos for six months. She knew other Australian girls over here and they all visited frequently. We got on wonderfully well together. Her boyfriend, when he came, was a knockout and they called in on us on the way home from their continental tour to bring gifts and disgorge the contents of the camper van they had bought in our garden. They sold the van but left all their gear with us. Very satisfactory all round!

My final choice proved fatal. I was very attracted to plump, bubbly Corinne, who knitted amazing garments for us all during her tenure. My husband told me he had an intuition she was somehow ominous when he first met her but was soon as used to having a laugh with her as we all were. She had had her problems – a baby in her teens who had been adopted and whom she mourned rather tipsily on various significant dates. But on the whole she had quite a zest for life and seemed very much to need to be part of our family. Unfortunately she carried this a little far and when I took a six month limited run theatre job in the West End, and was thus out every evening, she had an affair with my husband, thus justifying his clever presentiment. She had to go, of course, but things deteriorated later and our marriage broke up. My greatest satisfaction was throwing the Arran cricket sweater she had knitted for my husband out of the window into the rain. My children and I returned to Bedford to live near my parents who were a more than adequate substitute for their father most of the time. He and I remained friends and the children have always seen as much as they needed or wanted to of him. So we acquired a dog instead and my parents coped with the lot while I was working. So – no more Mother's Little Helpers!

Ah well, you can't win them all!

CAUSE CELEBRE – NEARLY

Some time in the nineteen eighties I did a television play for Anglia called "Cause Célèbre", based on the 1935 Rattenbury-Stonor case. The play included the murder itself and dwelled heavily on the lengthy proceedings of the trial, which was held at the Old Bailey in the Central Criminal Court. This last was quite an impressive set to construct and, due to the height of the court, could not be accommodated in the studios at Anglia so all the trial scenes were filmed in some studios at St Margaret's near Richmond and Twickenham. Helen Mirren was playing Alma Rattenbury and David Suchet the prosecuting council. To my shame I cannot remember the name of the young lad who played Stonor, but he was a pleasant fellow and a very good actor. I was playing the warder assigned to look after Alma Rattenbury. I sat with her in the box, having brought her up from below and remained with her throughout the trial. Such scenes as took place in the prison cell were done back in the studio at Norwich, and Helen and I also had two outside filmed scenes which I found rather frightening.

One took place in a sinister black car in which we were arriving at the Old Bailey. The case had created a good deal of interest at the time as Alma was a married woman who had been having an affair with the young Stonor, half her age, who had battered her husband to death. In fact, Stonor only became eighteen just before the trial. Throughout the trial she was vilified, more for this relationship than for the actual murder which she was accused of instigating. Thus there was a crowd outside the Old Bailey composed of supposed journalists, photographers and members of the public who mobbed us in a truly alarming way. The shouts, the faces at the window and the banging on the car were very realistic. Helen and I, sitting side by side in the back, both felt very strongly what it must be like to be actually in such a position. The scene had to be done several times of course and Helen and I formed quite a strong bond of sympathy as we waited and then repeatedly ran the gauntlet.

The second scary filming event was inside Norwich prison, when I escorted Helen out of a cell and along the walkway and down the stairs. There was just Helen, myself, the director and a hand-held camera man. It was a mute shot, which was just as well because the prisoners had been locked in their cells for the duration. They knew perfectly well that she was going to be there and kept up a perfect barrage of sound, battering on the doors and shouting Helen's name accompanied by varied and very imaginative comments. Once again we had a vivid impression of what it must be like to be them, and agreed the experience was somewhat unnerving. Although the comments were, on the whole, light-hearted there was an undercurrent of violence there.

I admired Helen's work very much and this was a great performance. She was an intelligent and jokey companion off the set when appropriate but her concentration when working is intense and in preparation for some of the emotional scenes in the witness box, like all good actors, she kept a wall of calm and silence around herself immediately prior to these scenes. I respected this unostentatious dedication and also her need to withdraw from the cast and crew at times when she could grab a rest period. The part was emotionally demanding and she always gives of her best.

Some months later I was surprised to receive a letter from a high-profile firm of London solicitors enclosing a copy of a page from a newspaper of more or less tabloid status. The article detailed some dispute between Anglia T.V. and Helen's agent over certain aspects of her contract, which had nothing to do with me. However it went on to vilify Helen, supposedly on the say-so of certain Anglia crew members. It stated that she was unfriendly, arrogant and very mush above her company and had generally behaved badly on the set. There were various details, to me evidently made up, either by the newspaper or by some technician who had fancied her, as they all did, and had probably over-stepped the line and been summarily dealt with by Helen, as she is very capable of doing. It is a perennial problem with her and she is a feisty lady. But I never heard her be unkind.

Helen was suing the newspaper and the solicitors requested that I should call at their office and give them a statement as to what I myself had seen and heard at the time. As my rôle had required my being at Helen's elbow throughout the trial I was uniquely placed to do so and I duly gave them a statement along the lines I have indicated as to my assessment of her talents, character and behaviour. The young actor playing Stonor, who had also been intimately associated with her in the play, likewise gave them a statement. They told me that David Suchet had also been asked to do so but, in spite of the fact that he had been very friendly with her and spent much time with her off the set, he had refused to do so. If I say that he was probably unwilling to offend Anglia T.V. by appearing to be on the other side of a dispute I am almost certainly libelling him!

After this I heard nothing further and was not called to give any evidence. Helen went back to America and I was left to presume that the case was settled out of court. I wondered about it on and off, and whether our statements had had any effect. I didn't see any further detractions of Miss Mirren in the Press.

But many months later, just before Christmas, I received a card from Helen and also a magnum of champagne which came in very handy for our New Year celebrations.

God bless "The Queen"!

FROM THE WINDOW

My children and I had found a small semi-detached house to live in. It had been eighteen months or so since we had left the conjugal home for good and we had been staying with my parents. Now we had been offered the chance to buy this house just around the corner from them and we were getting the feel of our surroundings. The house had no windows on the south side being semi-detached. The rooms upstairs and down had very pleasant aspects to east and west but on the north side there were again no windows – except one.

This was the small upstairs lavatory which had one narrow window, placed decently half way up the wall to preserve our modesty and, when we first moved in, I often used to linger surveying the somewhat restricted view to the side of our house: a glimpse of our garage roof, a dividing fence, part of a tree in the next door garden – nothing much in that. Much more tantalising was the vista through the side window of the next door house. A tall window, as befitted the large Victorian building, with dark velvet curtains, which were often not drawn until late at night, revealing the end wall of what was obviously the drawing room, and the door out to the hallway. Between the window and the door was a very handsome piece of furniture – an antique sideboard of inlaid dark wood, with glass doors suggesting a display of china in its hidden depths and on top some family photographs.

This scene was often brightly lit, focussing the eye upon it – the inmates were obviously prodigal with their electricity – and one particular photograph was angled in our direction. It showed a mother and two obvious daughters: one about the age of my own daughter, the other quite a bit younger. Both children were wearing dresses in a deep pink colour and they glowed giving the effect of people on a distant lighted stage.

From the tantalising sightings of an elderly lady – or were there two – making their entrances and exits through the door beyond I came to the conclusion that the cyclamen-robed pair in the photograph were probably beloved grand-children.

I knew that the little house next door was inhabited by at least one cantankerous lady of advanced years for she had emerged to make vigorous protests to our removal men when we were unloading our worldly goods. The driver had said to me,

"I don't envy you your neighbour, you'll have trouble there." I had not hastened to introduce myself therefore, and it was not until my daughter, walking on the flat garage roof and then bestriding the fence, made the acquaintance, as children will, of the very same older grand-daughter whose likeness I had been regarding with interest through my lofty spy-hole, that I was finally introduced to the occupants of my lighted drawing room. They proved to be twins, though not identical, in their sixties who lived one above the other in two flats, but were more often to be found together in the ground floor drawing room. They were a delightful couple and never gave me any of the predicted "trouble" although Eileen, the younger by half-an-hour or so, was addicted to protecting her rights vigorously and vocally against any imagined infringement. Molly, the elder with the husky voice of a constant smoker, was more likely to offer you a large whisky and both were indeed very generous with their hospitality.

It was the start of a friendship which lasted for twenty years or so, during which we came to know and love the entire family of children, grand-children, cousins and in-laws who often gathered in that spacious, high-ceilinged drawing room, especially at Christmas, when the photos on the sideboard were augmented by a host of cards and a poinsettia. We shared many such occasions with them and at New Year would emerge from our respective front doors with glasses of champagne in hand to first-foot each other's dwellings and sample each other's festive food.

Our close association continued even when Eileen suffered a series of strokes and became a wandering ghost in and out of that drawing room, with eyes fixed vacantly on some other world of her own. A friend and I visited every Wednesday without fail to have a drink and a chat with Molly and the various carers, while Eileen drifted back and forth or sat and reached constantly for her sister's hand. Sometimes she sat on her knee. This continued for nearly two years until the two of them, at some unspoken mutual signal, died within two days of each other. The last words I ever heard Molly say as she lay in bed with her eyes closed were to her carer:

"Give Gill a whisky. She likes ice with it. And bring one for me."

I miss them both more than I can say.

GOD DISPOSES

I am standing in the dining room of my parents' house, talking to my father as he puts cutlery away in the drawer after one of his customary washing-up sessions. I am feeling full of energy and excitement as I discuss with him my plans for changing my life-style and concentrating more seriously on my career. It is one of those moments of decision making where I remember exactly where I was and how I felt.

I had come back to live in Bedford with my two children after the break up of my marriage so that they had the full advantage of their adored grandparents' presence and warm support. We had taken some time establishing them in their new environment, and schools in particular, and enabling me to recover my equilibrium with the same firm support. My whole career had inevitably to go on a back burner. Although, through the kindness of a friend we had found a house just round the corner from my parents, thus enabling the children to use their own house but sleep at their grandparents if I had to be away for a day or two, I had mostly opted for short television engagements. I accepted whatever was most convenient for my situation, entirely for the money and regardless of the quality of the work. Twice during the decade of the eighties I ventured into limited theatrical enterprise, once at the National, which was repertoire, meaning one did not play continuously, and which was situated a convenient short walk from Blackfriars station on the Thameslink line; and the second time at Greenwich – a three-week run where I stayed very happily with an actress friend at Blackheath and walked across the park to work. Apart from this, work had rather deteriorated, particularly as I was at that late forties, early fifties age when actresses find out how very few good parts are written for them. Towards the end of the eighties the depression set in and my dear friend and agent, whom I had been with throughout my career, died, leaving me feeling bereaved and anchor-less.

So to my momentous discussions in the dining room with my father. I felt that I had to get back to my theatrical roots if I wanted my work to improve and be more fulfilling. A natural decision for an actress like me, nurtured in the old Repertory theatres and not a charismatic or "personality" actress, but what is usually termed a character actress, meaning that one can tackle a wide variety of differing roles with reasonable hope of success. I had had an offer from the National Theatre and to accept would not only revive my flagging career, as it is a splendid showcase and also a source of further work, but more importantly it would help me to become what is now termed 'my own person' again – that is an actress, and not just a mother. This was important in view of my advancing age and my feeling of being adrift in a much harsher and changing world of entertainment, without my agent and without the support of my theatrical friends from whom I was increasingly cut off, through not living in London.

This offer from the National seemed to have come at just the right time. It was a play I was very fond of: "Hedda Gabler", in a translation by Christopher Hampton. I had played "Thea Elvsted" in this version in 1970 in Stratford, Ontario and had come to know and admire the play profoundly. Now I was being asked to play "Aunt Julie" a smaller role but quite a challenge. I had shared a dressing room in Canada with an American actress, Ann Ives, who had often discussed with me the difficulties of the part, particularly in Aunt Julie's second scene, and I was keen to have a go. Juliet Stevenson would be playing Hedda, Howard Davies directing and it would, of course be in repertoire. There was to be an unusually long rehearsal period due to previous commitments of two of the cast and of Howard Davies himself who was directing another play at the National. This was fine as it would give me plenty of time for the part to sink into my consciousness and some time off to be with my family. The journey from Bedford to Blackfriars each day was a straightforward one and the brisk walk along the river to the theatre was, as I had found when doing "Major Barbara" there earlier in the decade, the perfect exercise before starting a day's rehearsal. This was to be the beginning of a new era of my life. I would do other plays afterwards and the theatre would give me back my artistic integrity in a way that television, fun though it can be, can never achieve for me.

Rehearsals were enjoyable, the company congenial and the part proved as fascinating as I had hoped. Howard Davies had some interesting ideas which added to my knowledge of, and respect for, the play and I was in sympathy with him and the cast, though that perfect ease with my character that has to be achieved was still eluding me. We had a refreshing interlude in our long rehearsal period when Melvyn Bragg decided to do a South Bank Show on Juliet Stevenson and to record part of my opening scene with her as part of this production. It was interesting to note how having a camera there subtly changed one's performance.

By Christmas time I had a bad cold and had developed a persistent cough and was experiencing some shortness of breath. After Christmas, when we resumed rehearsals, the cough was still there, my breathing was even worse affected and I had developed a pain in my shoulder. I finally managed to see my doctor in Bedford one evening and he ordered an X-Ray. I was getting worried, as the following week we were due to embark on a series of dress rehearsals and previews and I was feeling unaccountably tired. Earlier in the rehearsal period I had been concerned with a heavy feeling in my lower abdomen which I was afraid was due to a prolapsed womb, which had been mentioned as on the cards. A very young doctor at the gynae clinic had told me to go away and do exercises but I was not satisfied with this advice and my doctor had then ordered an ultra sound. I was told that I had fibroids and that they would have to be attended to but would not get any worse at present. I naturally reported this to Howard Davies who said that was fine, as long as I opened with the play and did a month or so with it, my part could be taken over while I had an op and I could even come back to it. This had all been put to the back of my mind and did not honestly occupy it at all at this later stage. Much more important to me was my restricted breathing and my deadly tiredness which was manifesting itself more and more upon the journey to work, although once I was at rehearsal I forgot about it. The day after my X-Ray the arduousness of the journey had assumed mammoth proportions. We did a run through of the play and to my joy my performance had suddenly risen to that plane where I knew that I had "got it" and that "it" would not now desert me. I travelled home and the stairs at Blackfriars seemed to go on and up for ever. I had to stop for breath several times and people were asking me if I felt alright. And I did, because the euphoria of the rehearsal remained with me. I struggled home and said to my father as I came off the train that I did not know quite how I was going to manage the journey again. He had come to fetch me and take me straight to the doctor's for the result of my X-Ray. I can still see that brightly lit room and experience the unreal quality that had come into my apprehension of my surroundings. The doctor told me that I had a pleural effusion; my lung was full of fluid and I must go straight into hospital the next morning.

The following week is a jumble in my memory. The desperate worry about the play, the phone calls from the theatre to the hospital, the trapped sensation, the awful pain of the draining of the fluid and the absolute agony of the attempt to dig out a bit of my lung for biopsy, when the nurse told me to hold her hands and shout if I wanted to – I was in a side ward – while the doctor dug into my back. I availed myself freely of her permission and collapsed exhausted for the rest of the day. Then the moment when I spoke with Howard on the phone and it was decided that my part must be taken over by someone else – a horrific proposition as they were about to go into dress rehearsals. The unfortunate actress turned out to be a great friend of mine who was much smaller than I, and had to be found a new costume, although she told me later that we had the same size head so the wig was alright. Then, with the loss of hope for the immediate future came the releasing of tension, the acceptance, the flowers and letters from the company, the recuperation, then the severance from those people and that project that had filled my life over a period of three months. Then the discharge from hospital, the blankness of prospect, taking me off to the gynae clinic, "We wondered what had happened to you!" The examination, and the second nightmare begins: "You must come into hospital for an operation the day after tomorrow." "I am sorry, but this could be very serious: very serious indeed."

He didn't believe in pulling his punches, my consultant, when I finally got to see him. I knew what he meant. He was quite certain that I had cancer and that the diagnosis was very late and the prognosis not too hopeful. The fluid in my lungs had arrived there from my lower regions, where all hell had broken loose. Ovarian cancer, the silent killer, was well advanced there. I told my parents what he had said, but they hadn't actually heard him, and persisted in believing that this was just a hypothesis. I knew it was a certainty but I just wanted to sit quietly by myself and not absorb it. The strange dream like quality persisted over the interim before I went into hospital. My mind had accepted what he said but my emotions were on hold. I went through my daily routine mechanically but I just wanted to sit very still, and by myself. Not to talk to anyone: just keep very quiet and very, very still so that I did not disturb the monster inside me and make it angry. In my state of almost suspended animation it might ignore me and go away. And time – I was holding back time by my quietness and solitude. Nothing could happen – there was only that endless moment in time.

The realities of hospital routine and the preparations for an operation were welcome in that they provided an occupation and a preoccupation, "Just live for the moment", is the advice, once cancer has been diagnosed. I seemed to do this automatically in the early stages because my mind couldn't, or didn't, wish to encompass the future. Later, of course, I understood the advice. There are such long periods of inactivity, of allowing therapy to work, of just awaiting outcomes that impatience is useless and can only be self-destructive. I arrived for the operation almost in a state of trance. It was just before Valentine's Day, and I remember I bought two for my children and tried to give them each a message of undying love. It seemed somehow important.

After the operation the consultant came round, surrounded by his minions, and murmured, "It was what we thought it was." He then explained that he had taken away everything in sight that was remotely removable, hysterectomy wise, in an effort to contain the disaster. Chemotherapy would be discussed later. I sat in my chair by the window in my side room – they get you out of bed pretty early – and felt nothing further than tiredness and feelings of relief that the op was over. I noticed a nurse, who had already become "my favourite nurse" in that she managed to be both efficient and busy and to convey sympathy, glancing in several times at me through my open door as she bustled past. Finally she came in and sat down, and asked me how I was feeling. I realised that she was asking about my reactions to the news that the consultant would have broken to me, not realising that he had already convinced me three days before and that I had been going through my reactions, or non-reactions, ever since. But I was still an actress and I immediately responded as the scene required and reproduced some symptoms so that she could offer comfort. A lot of people think that this is typical actor's behaviour and shows insincerity or hypocrisy. This is untrue. The feelings I had were real. I produced them for her at this moment because I liked her and sensed her sympathy and her desire to comfort. This made her happy and I was happy and helped by her warmth and humanity. Satisfaction all round.

Life in hospital is only bearable if you immerse yourself in the life around you: the routine, the other patients, the nurses, the doctors' rounds, even the food. You have to distance yourself from your outside life; otherwise you will be unhappy and restless. I learned this when I had to be hospitalised for three months before the birth of my daughter. The only other place I have experienced this detachment from normal life and intensity of the immediate environment is on board a ship. The month that I now spent in hospital proved to be a useful cut-off point between my attempted career-renewal and the future. I accepted that I had a new temporary goal which was to deal with this illness and the even more frightening, because more immediate, "cures" proposed. There were plenty of people in the ward to regale me with horror stories about the dreaded 'chemotherapy' and its results. I was to have my first taste of this at the end of my month in hospital and looked forward with a great deal of trepidation to the event. I was not to go to Addenbrook's, which was then the normal place to go, but to receive treatment here in the gynae ward from doctors who were as unfamiliar with the process as I was, but were under instruction from Addenbrook's and as eager to undergo the experience as I was not!

This experience of chemotherapy, I have to explain, was very different from what it is now, and from what I encountered five years later when my hostilities were resumed. A different drug was used, not at all a pleasant one, a cis-platin instead of carbo-platin I think, but I may be wrong. You would not think names once engraved on my heart would have fled my memory now, would you? The process was also much more prolonged and entailed the passing of buckets of fluid through my system for hours before and after the drug was administered. This was to save my poor kidneys from annihilation, which was a likely outcome apparently.

So, back to my side ward, and a nightmare forty-eight hours or so. I was very alone in the darkened room – nurses checked me regularly but were too busy to linger. To make things worse, there was a bad storm outside which made the room as dark during the day as the night and kept up a persistent noise of wind, rain and thunder most trying to the nerves. It turned out later that they had miscalculated the amount or the strength of the anti-sickness drug I was given and, though I was not sick as I Had expected, this drug had the effect of giving me strange spasms in my tummy area for some time as it was coming in to effect and later, when it was wearing off, and just as the nurses were urging me to sleep, as the worst was over, it produced similar spasms in my back making sleep impossible.

This dosage was adjusted when I had my second – and as it turned out last – session a month later. This time I was sick, or at least did a lot of retching at intervals which I found preferable to the previous occasion and was even proud of myself that I, who had always experienced difficulty in being sick and found it a frightening and painful affair, had now mastered the techniques of it and would henceforth fear no more. But on that second occasion the sun was shining outside, the room was quiet but light, I had no spasms and I had done it all before and worked out how to cope.

But, back in my darkened room on the first occasion, I experienced all the symptoms of a bad attack of 'flu after the cis-platin was administered and the spirit-breaking thing was that these terrible fluids were still relentlessly coursing through my system and my bladder was incessantly crying out for relief. The little side room had an attached lavatory but the nurses soon fortunately realised that it seemed like a million miles away to me, and placed beside my bed, a commode. In any case I had to use the horrible cardboard receptacles for urine that now obtain in our hospitals. These were given to me in a stack and the bastards get stuck inside one another and refuse to come apart especially when one hand is occupied with a drip on a stand and one's head is not helping either. Each of these receptacles had to be placed ready for intermittent nurse collection as every precious drop had to be weighed in the balance against my fluid intake. I don't know what they thought I might be doing with it, or where they thought I might be secreting it in between. All I wanted in my flu-like state was to lie there and suffer and the mental effort to flagellate my poor limbs into getting out of bed so frequently left me weary and tearful.

Enough! Draw a veil.

GOD CONTINUES TO DISPOSE

I was supposed to be having my chemotherapy at the end of the month for six months but I never got beyond the first two. When I went for my check up before the April session it was decided that my kidneys would not take any more. Instead I was to try some pills – I've forgotten their name now. I would take them for fourteen days at the beginning of each month and would go across the road to the gynae clinic at the North Wing each month to be checked out.

Suddenly all the frantic hospital life was on hold and I was left with that blank feeling as you try to get your life going again. First of all I needed a little holiday and my thoughts turned inevitably to Southwold. Our house had been sold by then of course, but the family one of my cousins had married into owned a small cottage there and this proved to be available. I went for a week and my husband elected to come to look after me. At that time we had a legal separation but were not divorced and he visited us regularly at Christmas and other holiday times. We had a very peaceful and happy week there relaxing and taking me for a little longer walk each day. The weather was brilliantly sunny and my husband fed me on beautifully cooked fresh fish. On one day he paid seven pounds for some turbot.

Returned home, I settled into my new regime and eventually went back to work gratefully accepting a small role in "Waiting for God" which my dear friend Steff Cole had suggested me for. A further success occurred when I was asked to do a Christmas Special in the television T-bag series which I had first experienced the year before. I really enjoy doing children's programmes like this, it is a bit like pantomime – and I was able to follow up my brilliant performance as Hazel Nut with a triumphant Emily Sweet. Both these programmes I have on videotape and are a regular favourite with youthful visiting children.

Work had been seriously interrupted however and offers were sparse and not always possible to accept for health reasons. Enter my life then "The Chief". I had watched the first series on telly and enjoyed it, particularly as I very much admire Tim Piggott-Smith then playing the lead. In the first series he had had a personal secretary played by a local Norwich girl – it was an Anglia production – but it had been decided they needed somebody more experienced for the role, which although bitty required a quietly sympathetic and efficient personality able to make its own impact. The fact that she was never required for filming, being anchored to the office, and that the part was fairly sedentary just suited my convalescent requirements. I have always loved Norwich and particularly enjoyed working for Anglia, which had an almost homelike quality with local drivers with cosy Norfolk accents ferrying you about even when you were only going to the studio (a courtesy peculiar to Anglia alone). The crews and the wardrobe and make up artists were equally friendly and involved themselves in our concerns.

For the next four years this series saved my life. It gave me purpose, a feeling of achievement and a host of new friends. Tim was replaced in the third series by Martin Shaw whom I came equally to love and admire. The second in command or A.C.C, was played by Karen Archer. She and I shared a flat in Norwich and she was the greatest support to me at all times, travelling a long way to visit me when I had to go back to hospital and sharing with me her lovely family of actor husband and twins – one of each sex. The friendly drivers would sometimes arrive early and share our breakfast and the news of the day, local and national, with us. The clever wardrobe mistress reconciled me to the fact of going up a size when I recovered from the operation thinness and the steroids kicked in. She introduced me to Ann Harvey clothes for the larger woman, dressed me imaginatively and allowed me to buy outfits after use at a greatly reduced cost. Penny, my favourite make-up artist, gave me camomile tea to drink in the early mornings, came to eat with us sometimes in the evening and later, when I lost my hair, spent a good hour after working hours trimming and shaping my National Health wig into something resembling a human hairdo. For the show itself she had a wig made to look like the Polaroid pictures she had of my own hair and when the series ended, quietly gave this to me along with a lovely old wig block and a page of instructions on wig care. This was something of a defiant gesture as Anglia had just been taken over in those sweeping television company reforms that also swept away Thames Television where my husband worked. Penny lost her job because she was a supervisor and cost them more than a more junior make-up girl which would be all they required in the future as they did not intend to do any more of the brilliant and unusual drama programmes (such as Tales of the Unexpected and the P.D. James mysteries) for which they had been well known. The last bastion of the caring, interested and interesting old T.V. companies, who made you feel part of a family, was lost to us.

Who but Anglia would have treated me as they did when, in 1993, my C.A.125 count went right up again and a scan confirmed I had to have another operation. The cancer, still identifiable as ovarian cells, had reappeared in an interesting part of the anatomy of which I had never heard, known as the pouch of Douglas! This exciting area is situated somewhere low down amongst all the tangle of bladder, bowels etc in these regions. A little oasis of nothingness, just right for a questing cancer cell to make its home in. This time the surgeon managed to remove 95% of the offending growth, the remaining 5% having attached itself to bits of me I might be going to need later. But it was small and so I was told that this was the time for radiotherapy. For this I would have to go back to Addenbrook's in Cambridge. So I duly trotted off for the first session where the doctor assesses the mount of radiotherapy you need and how it is to be spread over how much time, and in what amounts. To my surprise the doctor said that she thought it would be more appropriate for me to have chemotherapy. I explained what I had had, and how it had been discontinued but she told me that it was all different now and that she felt it was my best course. At least I would be able to have it back in Bedford.

I found that it was indeed different and started a regime in which the actual treatment took only half an hour or so, but the whole day still had to be devoted to the enterprise as you had to wait a couple of hours first to see a doctor to confirm your readiness to go ahead, and then more hours waiting for your turn at the actual treatment. I think they had room, and nurses, to treat two at a time, or it might have been three at most, and the waiting room was frighteningly full. Unlike any other clinic at that time, there were no complaints about the waiting. People were in varying stages of illness, some in wheelchairs, some walking with difficulty, many hairless, all pale and tired looking. But there was always someone worse than oneself and everybody knew that this treatment was their only hope so they brought sandwiches and books to read or chatted quietly to each other. I made several friendships there and one woman, who'd also had ovarian, used to ring me up at home and enquire how I was, or occasionally meet me in the town and compare notes. I had her number too, but when she finally ceased to ring I hadn't the courage to phone and enquire about her. At the end of these sessions my C.A.125 count was still not satisfactory and I was eventually asked if I would care to go to Addenbrook's to join the latest programme trying out the effect of a brand new drug called Taxol, which was apparently made from the bark of the Pacific Yew tree and cost several thousands a dose. This was an all day session and you lay on a bed with a very slow drip which first delivered you a fair dose of steroids before the Taxol. This on top of a dose of twenty little white steroid pills which you took the night before, so it was fair to say that the drug was regarded as pretty poisonous one way and another. This is when I began to get seriously moon faced and finally lost all my hair. The treatment was once every four weeks and none of the nurses liked me because my hand refused to yield up suitable veins without great difficulty and they finally had to use my wrist which they were not supposed to do. The camaraderie amongst the patients was intense and we all became involved with each other's lives and families as the results became increasingly dramatic in reduction of our C.A.125 count.

I had been offered the fifth series of "The Chief" at this time and was able to accept through the kindness of Anglia and the director who arranged that my scenes should all be done in the last week before my next treatment when I was feeling the least ill effects of this very debilitating process. This was possible because my scenes all took place within the office complex set which was erected in order to do all relevant scenes consecutively. They weren't, of course, consecutive in the finished episode but it is the cheapest and easiest way to organise the shooting. The journey to Norwich presented me with some problems as it can only be done via St Pancras and Liverpool Street and I wasn't fit to carry much luggage. I arranged for a local taxi firm to take me there for the first session. It was costly but I felt I had no choice. Dear Martin

Shaw asked me how I got there and then went off and saw the powers that be, who thereafter sent a car for me each month, there and back. I was very grateful both to Martin and to them. I enjoyed the series very much on the whole, although when I catch a repeat on Sky I am very much aware of my characteristic steroid moon face, which brings some of the worst features back to me.

My mother was wonderfully supportive of me during this time, as I was trying to be of her because on the day on which my scan results had confirmed the return of my cancer, and the necessity for my second operation, my father had suffered an unexpected and severe heart attack and had died next day in intensive care without regaining consciousness. It had been a traumatic time for us all as he was a very special person and my children also were both severely affected by his loss. However, we were all living in my parents' home by this time in order to pool our financial resources owing to my restricted earning ability and the four of us helped each other through 1994 with all its problems and new experiences.

However, in November of this year my mother, who had had no more warning than the occasional dizzy spell, fell victim to the brain tumour which had been quietly growing. It seemed that one week she was doing the Times Crossword with me, and two weeks later she couldn't find her way alone to the bathroom. So it seemed that God hadn't finished his disposal of our lives quite yet. But maybe I shall leave the final chapter of this dismal saga, which nevertheless included a great deal of humour and love and those famous learning curves, to another session.

GOD FINALLY STOPS DISPOSING
AND ALLOWS US TO PROPOSE AGAIN

Christmas of that year of 1994, soon after my mother's tumour had made itself manifest, was a surprisingly cheerful one. For this my Mother herself was largely responsible being in remarkably light hearted mood. Her memory had been affected in the best possible way, distancing her from the loss of my father and revealing a gay and humorous side to her character we had not entirely suspected. She was like a child again and, as such, seemed to enjoy the festive season. My husband joined us and the family were able to enjoy a brief respite from care, happy in the knowledge that the Taxol had brought about a dramatic reduction in my C.A.125 count.

The New Year, however, saw the climax of the saga, my Mother's mood and capabilities deteriorating sharply and my dramatic improvement gradually eroding. My Mother still made us laugh quite often with her fantasies about George Aligayah and her indignation about the Germans which I described elsewhere. But she was physically weakening, she needed a catheter and she was becoming impossible for me to manoeuvre let alone lift, even with my daughter's staunch support. Enter a wonderful Macmillan nurse called Ella who supported us all, arranged visits from district nurses, attendance allowance for Mum and Disability Living Allowance for me and also step forward St John's Hospice at Moggerhanger which gave us all respite care and finally admitted my Mother for the last time to care for her lovingly until her death in March, two days after my birthday. They embraced the whole family and went on doing so after she had died sending invitations to memorial services at the local church and sending me, memorably, a multi-signed Get-Well card when I later went back into hospital. I once asked a nurse there how they all managed to offer so much outgoing affection to their patients given that these were all terminal cases. She said, "Well there are a great many of us to share the emotional involvement, and we don't go on doing the job for too many years." They were able to identify the day that would be mother's last – St Patrick's Day – ringing me in the morning, when she had been in a coma for a week, saying they had "noticed a change". Only their experience would have done so and it meant that I was able to sit beside her all day, and well into the evening, talking sometimes out loud, thinking a great deal, touching her gently and adjusting myself quietly to her loss. Late in the evening a nurse who was going back to Bedford persuaded me to go with her and it was a measure of my confidence in the love and care surrounding her there, that I was able to do so without guilt. She died in the early hours of the next morning.

The funeral and a certain amount of clearing up over, I was able to take a short holiday with my cousin Sue in her peaceful Cornwall home before returning to hospital for a laparoscopy, presided over by two surgeons each holding a watching brief for their own particular areas of expertise. The outcome of this was that I was handed over by my now good friend, Mr Ogborn the gynaecologist, to Mr Foley who was henceforth to be in charge of my bowels and my wayward digestive system altogether. The cancer, obviously unhappy with its rather boring home in my prettily named pouch of Douglas had elected to opt for the busy world of the intestines and a colostomy was prescribed. This entailed another wait during which I went back to Cornwall armed with copious information on the proposed alterations to my system, including a video, in which John Cleese, with great energy and verve, and the visual evidence provided by several colostomates (as I later learned to call them) endeavoured to persuade me that the whole thing was the very latest, highly desirable fashion, and indeed the only way to live!

Not over persuaded I returned to hospital on May 20th, my Mother's birthday, and embarked on the whole process of clearing out the entire digestive system in every possible exciting way, then surgery, recovery and the fascinating procedure for Living with a Stoma – into which I do not propose going in any detail. Suffice it to say that the embonpoint which I was carrying on my tummy made it rather a long journey for my truncated intestine to reach the outside world and the stoma itself was not as neatly accomplished as they would have wished it to be. Indeed, Mr Foley's registrar, a tall rather humourless Sikh, who had obviously not yet come to terms with western ideas of the emancipated position of women, wanted to haul me back into theatre and start all over again, but kind Mr Foley felt that I had had enough surgery for the time being and was confident that I could make it work. Which, with varying success, I have done ever since. My time in hospital was made possible, and even at times pleasant, by the wonderful stoma care nurse (since re-titled, unprettily, colo-rectal nurse) Jude Cottam, a small energetic and dedicated person, who walked the wards in high heels, the sound of whose brisk tapping lightened the spirits of us all whenever we heard it. As my neighbour in the ward whispered, when Jude returned from a spell of off-duty, "Hooray, Aslan's back in Narnia!" This neighbour, Gina, became a life-long friend and together we supported each other's spirits by indulging in a great deal of childish humour and, I may say, a few communal tears, comforted by being shared. Gina was insistent that we should name our stomas since they had become temporarily the most important things in our lives. She was going to name hers Piglet because he was "a friend of Poo(h)!" I decided that as mine had turned out rather clumsy I should call it Heffalump. These appellations delighted us both and cheered us on our way considerably. Unfortunately Gina's Piglet proved not to solve her problem and she was later taken into hospital for an Iliostomy. This involves removing the large intestine altogether and tapping into the small intestine. This is okay because it is the small intestine that absorbs most of the essential nourishment, the large intestine's function being mostly to absorb all the liquid. Without this activity the liquid remains and the ileostomy is consequently more lively and fountain like. Gina mourned the loss of her Piglet and so to cheer her up I sent her a black edged funeral card for Piglet and in the same envelope a congratulatory one on the birth of "Tigger". These names have remained with us to this day and Tigger has proved as bouncy as his namesake whilst dear old Heffalump is as gauche and unwieldy as ever.

When I was released from hospital after the added complication of a burst wound and an abscess, I was eventually sent to Addenbrook's for a course of radiotherapy. This time it did actually happen and proved eventually to put the final full stop to my saga – well for the last eleven years anyway. The treatment was trying in itself and the daily journey to Cambridge a bit of a nightmare, in spite of the splendid voluntary drivers who augment the ambulance services so nobly. The trouble is that one's own treatment last's approximately a minute and a half, but if one is sharing transport with, say, a dialysis patient, it's an all day job. It was a very hot August too. However it eventually appeared to have done the trick and so it was worth every airless, jolting journey.

I didn't do a great deal of work after this. The following year I had my sixtieth birthday and attained my state pension. Coupled with my continuing disability allowance this was at least a means to live. Jobs were few and far between considering the long gaps I had had and my general debility, and if I worked I would have to forfeit my disability allowance without definite prospects for my next job. The needs of my colostomy coupled with a bladder weakened by surgery made me rather unfit for television jobs which almost always involved filming with usually very primitive sanitary arrangements.

I went to some interviews and did the odd job during the next year, notably doing the radio version of "As Time goes by" which I had done for telly. This was recorded in the lovely little thirties decorated theatre at the BBC in Langham Place, with an audience. I hadn't worked in this theatre before and I enjoyed both this and the reunion with Judi Dench and with Geoffrey Palmer, an old friend of mine. But in 1997, after a trip to do a couple of small scenes with Jessica Lange in Balzac's "Cousin Bette" in Bordeaux when my luggage was lost, complete with necessary colostomy gear, I decided to call it a day. Being a film there was, of course a French doctor attached to the unit who took a sample of what I needed from my hand luggage to the local chemists and managed to come up with identical gear for me. But my confidence was shaken and it was enough. Both financially and medically it was sensible for me to retire gracefully and embark on the huge adventure of finding out about the Real World and what Normal People do with their Lives.

More of this ongoing epic anon.

NEW BEGINNINGS

And so the year 2007 dawns quietly for me, and it will be ten years since I made my decision to retire, more or less gracefully, from a career which had absorbed most of my thoughts and energies for forty-one years. I made no New Resolutions except perhaps, once again, to drink less whisky which I cannot afford either physically or financially. Mine were all made in that year of 1997 and have been an ongoing project ever since. What did I have? I had a reprieve from my illness.

I had my Life Membership of Equity, gained for putting in forty of those years, and my memories; I had some very dear friends, whom I saw less of since my move to Bedford, but we were all very articulate on the telephone; and I had my two children and lately the almost perfect partners they have picked for themselves. I had my parents' old home in which to live, bursting at the seams with happy memories. But who was I? I had spent so many years getting under the skin of so many different roles – and let's face it, even as a mother I had treated the experience as my most important and sustained performance in which it was vital to succeed – that I had had no time to discover if there was a real me with definite opinions and characteristics.

So I had to re-invent myself in what might turn out to be my last and greatest presentation – Retirement. I knew I should experience withdrawal symptoms, but felt instinctively that my new life should not at first include the theatre or any knowledge of what was going on in the profession. Things had been changing so rapidly there in recent years that I already felt alienated from a world with fewer provincial theatres and a West End more and more devoted to lavish musicals. The drama schools too had changed their character, life was real and earnest, competition was keen, new skills had to be developed; the computer age was well and truly with us.

Had I any place in this new world? Any other skills? What were my interests? Well, reading. And, of course, people. I had already become part of a community at St Andrew's Church where, during my illness I had joined a group which included elderly, ill and disabled people who met on Wednesday mornings in the Holt room for a communion service followed by tea, coffee, scones and chat. Birthdays were celebrated with signed cards, cakes with icing and candles, and song. There was a special Christmas lunch. These people and their friendship became very important to me. Other things followed through the church, such as people in local retirement homes to whom I could go and read poems and stories; recorded readings for the blind and a weekly session for the very pre-school young, called Noah's Ark, where I could try my skills at holding the attention of two and three-year-olds with Bible Stories, when they would much rather be still banging drums and tambourines and singing "The wheels on the bus …."

But was this the path to continued mental agility and fulfilment? My aunt and uncle had tried to interest my mother in Bedford's wonderful Retirement Education Centre, with which they were very actively involved, but she had preferred to sit at home in comfort and read and do the crossword. Now seemed to be the moment to examine the resources of this much vaunted palace of enlightenment. The inmates had just won their battle to keep the place alive after it no longer had council funding. The establishment had been taken over, funding and all, by the people it served, a new administration was at the helm and a bright new future promised. As well as the courses offered by the Centre itself there were Cambridge Courses under the auspices of Madingley College. The new world was opening up before me.

That first autumn term, with an embarrass de richesses spread before me, I finally chose a course on the Celts, and one by Graham Howes on "Religion Myth and Ritual". Both were fascinating and absorbing experiences but the choice of Graham's course was particularly fortuitous as it was he who persuaded me that I had finally found a valid new and exciting direction for my life. I did every one of his courses each year until he himself retired and left us. He was, broadly speaking a social anthropologist with a wide experience of world cultures and religions – he had worked for the Archbishop of Canterbury at one time. He was also something of a bon viveur, knowledgeable about wines and food and offered us one captivating course on food and drink world-wide and how it reflected national character and custom. But his chief attribute was the way he treated every small verbal contribution by every one of us with complete and serious interest. He, more than anyone, gave me a sense of my value as a thinking person and member of the community. I was beginning to believe in a persona quite apart from my acting ability. The knowledge he imparted to me was vast and various but the most valuable thing he gave me was a sense of self, and even of self-worth.

Meanwhile I was backing up my new found discovery of the real world with other courses. I did one or two terms of "General Studies" which were simply a series of lectures by visiting people, rather in the style of the W.I. but with an added masculine input, on all the institutions and hobbies and alternative careers which I ought to have known something about and hadn't in my previous life. "The Celts" had been an archaeology-based course and I did one or two others but rather cut them out later on account of my legs not being too good for field trips. I avoided any courses to do with the theatre, or even literature, gave a nod towards art history, but left music severely alone as my ignorance there is vast. Religion continued to be a theme, though I baulked a bit at Buddhism and went off at a tangent to Scottish Castles. But fairly early on I came inevitably to Philosophy, in spite of many misgivings, and there I have stuck. Again, we had a brilliant but very different tutor in Richard Mason: intelligent, witty enigmatic but intriguing – like his subject. I have managed to grasp that Philosophy is not going to give me any answers but simply raise interesting questions and perhaps this is what I want. There is a circle of people who have stuck with the subject from the beginning and they have become my friends. I would go to the classes just to be with and listen to them even if the Philosophy palled, but it doesn't. In the summer term we continue to get together as a group and worry at all the old questions with ageing but tenacious teeth.

And so to my writers' group: all such friends. I seem to have known them for years. We don't have a lot of secrets from one another but seem to get on well just the same. By writing about it I have connected back to my past and have a feeling of coming full circle. I look forward to our sessions, and being entrusted with the private thoughts and emotions of so many different characters.

I can sincerely say that I now enjoy my life very much and am able to view my fellow actors on television, and occasionally on the stage, without envy. So much so that in recent years, with the encouragement of my dear friend Elizabeth Goddard, whose training and professional life have paralleled mine and means that we understand each other completely, I have overcome my reluctance to "perform" again and have taken part in various entertainments with an ease and enjoyment that are quite new to me. I don't do learning any more, but I enjoy readings of both prose and poetry. I don't feel it is "showing off" but a simple celebration and appreciation of other people's written work.

Do I know who I am now? Probably not. I am just content to be a person whom my new friends seem to like to be with, doing things that interest us and that we like to do.

GUILTY CONSCIENCE

It's a well-known, well-worn, saying that conscience makes cowards of us all. Shakespeare was alluding to the increased fear of death of those with guilty sins on their conscience, and blames it for Hamlet's inertia. Oliver Goldsmith agreed that conscience is a coward and added,

"those faults it has not strength enough to prevent, it seldom has justice enough to accuse."

Well maybe. I know that there is one bit of writing I have known I should include in my jumbled account of people and places which have meant something in my life, but I have always shied away from it. I told myself that I could not do the subject justice and that my memories were too insubstantial and yet too precious to be recorded with my lack of skill. Yet the pieces I wrote about my dear friend Jean, both for her funeral and later for the writing group, were very helpful to me in my grief at her loss; likewise the affectionate memories of Molly and Eileen, who latterly took the place of my parents. But Pauline? What is stopping me is guilt. I feel I betrayed her at the end of her life and as I can do nothing about it now I have tried to forget it. But perhaps I owe it to her to make the attempt to write. My inadequacies were well known to her and never affected her friendship.

She was always known to my parents, during the thirty or more years she worked for them, as Mrs Shaw and indeed, even though she asked me in her latter years to call her Pauline I always thought of her as Mrs Shaw, despite our increasing intimacy as I grew older and launched out on the world. When she first came to us she had a daughter (by a previous marriage) of eleven or so, a husband quite a bit younger than her and a new son, Philip, in a pram, who lay contemplating our garden from that haven as she worked. She was a very efficient and practical lady – she had been in the wrens during the war – and was a great complement domestically to my more irresolute and gentle mother. Mum did have definite ideas on how she wanted things to be done in her home but was less decided on the practical details of how they should be carried out. Mrs Shaw, brimming with energy, would cut through all the red tape, as it were, and whilst Mum was still discussing possibilities, she would have rolled up her sleeves and got on with what she saw to be the next thing to be done. She had plenty of initiative, which might have been a problem were it not for the enormous admiration she had for my mother, whom she thought was a real lady. She told me later that she always had a picture of my mother going out to catch a bus into Bedford in a summer dress, wearing not only a hat but also little white gloves. She was very impressed by these gloves, which became some sort of a symbol to her. She and my mother got on very well, as she was intelligent, with a sense of humour and a great willingness to oblige those whom she respected. She quickly became indispensable to us and an integral part of all family festivities and, indeed, calamities. She was most truly a friend, but she was still Mrs Shaw. She never asked my mother to call her Pauline. I think it was something to do with the white gloves.

As she followed up Philip in quick succession with three other children, there was a time when the youngest were still pre-school when she did not come to clean for us for two or three years, although she visited us as a friend, and we had to suffer the ministrations of the lady whom my father always referred to as "Mrs Darlow-whom-God-preserve", because she required all our Christian charity and patience to cope with her low I.Q. She was very well meaning but made the sort of remarks that there is no answer to and perpetrated many blunders, such as consigning my 21st birthday gold watch to the incinerator. We all heaved a sigh of relief when Mrs Shaw came back to us and effortlessly resumed her paramount position in our family.

She had her troubles. Her daughter, Jean, became pregnant in her teens and had the support of her mother, but the baby had severe Downs Syndrome and only lived for two years. He had to live in a home and Jean visited him there constantly, but after he died her mother thought she could do with a change of scene, particularly as her siblings were all so young and noisy, and sent her to live with her grandmother in Southport which was her own town of origin. They were a typical northern family, very earthy, as Pauline was herself. She told me that when she had milk fever when breast feeding Jean, her grandmother had used a cow-pat as poultice, which proved very efficacious. Jean obviously felt more comfortable with her Lancashire roots and remained there, eventually marrying and having a family of determined northerners.

Her step-father, Terry, was a southerner and drove long-distance lorries for a living. He was a friendly soul, rather good looking, and would sometimes turn up in a town where I was working in the theatre and take me out to some cafe where we would both indulge in his favourite meal of a very large and greasy comprehensive fry-up. In view of this it was no surprise when, in later years, he developed heart trouble and could no longer drive heavy goods vehicles. There was some trouble with his eyes as well. But whatever his habits had been on his long distance journeys, when he was finally confined to base, as it were, in Kempston, he committed the crowning folly of indulging in an affair with a younger woman. For this Pauline never forgave him. She had her principles and family came first with her so she never turned him out, but as far as she was concerned their relationship was dead. Her children were fond of him – he was a fairly lovable character – but their home became a place where their mother only spoke to their father about necessary, practical things, and made her large contempt for him continually obvious. She was a very strong character and held the home together in an admirable way. All her children turned out, as they say, very well and appeared essentially undamaged.

The lack of a warm marital relationship, I think, caused her to become increasingly involved with our family who loved her and she felt would never let her down.

When I eventually had a family she was always there at every crisis and, her own children being by then much older, she would leave home to come and stay with me. When I had to move house she was there helping me sort and pack and with typical ruthlessness getting rid of all my sixties clothes which my daughter would later have given her eye-teeth for, in her costume shop. I was a far less decided person, domestically, that my mother and Pauline organised my household with affectionate firmness. I was the more surprised then to discover, when she was staying with me in Teddington, that this gallant woman, who had been through the war, was afraid of thunderstorms. I had to sit up with her one night drinking tea during a storm.

When I came back to live in Bedford and had a house round the corner from my parents she was in her element. She would come from cleaning for them to deal inexorably with my household needs, which included painting as well as cleaning and, of course, throwing out all the things, useless in her eyes, which I tended to hang on to. I would give her lunch seated companionably in the dining room or, weather permitting, out on the terrace where she once delighted my children by slowly keeling over backwards in her deck chair to land full length on the lawn. It was the slow motion effect and the slight look of surprise on her face that set them laughing whenever they thought of it. It was at this epoch that she asked me to call her Pauline, which I did with difficulty but she remained Mrs Shaw to my children as to my parents.

She had always said to me that I was not to worry about my mother as she would look after her for me, so it was quite a shock when it was she herself who suddenly crumbled. She was ill for a few weeks with some undefined illness and when we finally went over to her house to see her we found that her legs seemed to have ceased working properly, and she had to crawl upstairs on her hands and knees. We never found out exactly what was the matter with her – she herself seemed very vague – and I had a feeling that her very active and often stressful life had simply worn her out. But it was obvious she wasn't coming back to us.

Soon after this, came the period of my own illness and, eventually, my parent's deaths. We didn't see that much of her – she didn't seem to want us to visit and when we did there was a constraint that had never been there before. She was a very different woman from the one we had all known and loved. She seemed content to stay at home with the now faithful Terry whose affection for her was very obvious. And as her sharp tongue was now totally blunted there was a new feeling of harmony between them. Her children, who now had young families of their own, were very attentive and she seemed to sink back into her own family circle. We missed her, of course, but were very much occupied with our own troubles at this era.

She came to my mother's funeral and was with our family in the front pew. Afterwards she made her final trip over to my parent's house to help me clear out my mother's clothes. She said they were the hardest, because most intimately personal, effects one had to deal with and she wanted to sort them reverently because, "Your mother always took so much care of her clothes." At her request I gave her my mother's vests and nightdresses because she said that whenever she requested presents of underwear from her family they always said that was dull and gave her something else she didn't want. That was the last time she came to our house.

There followed a time when my life seemed to be very busy and I never managed to get over to Kempston to see her. She seemed to have vanished strangely from our lives. Then one day Terry rang me to say she was in Bedford hospital and he didn't think she would be coming out. I went to see her and was able to talk to her and to know that she recognised me and murmured a few words from behind her oxygen mask. I did tell her how much I loved her and made a few of the feeble sort of jokes we had shared as one does in these impossible situations. I went home feeling very sad, and Terry rang to say she had died two days later.

And then – I missed her funeral. I don't know why I expected her family to let me know. There was apparently a notice in the local paper a few days after she died but I never read it. The days passed and I found out that it had already happened – quite quickly for once. I was horrified because I knew her family would see it as an inexplicable lack of respect for her memory and all she had done for us. I was so stricken with guilt that I was never able to muster the courage to phone Terry and I couldn't decide what to write in a letter, so I left it until it was impossible to say anything, and I haven't seen her family since.

I still can't believe that it all happened in that way, and my guilt at my neglect of her at the end of my life is enormous. Incidentally, my mother had always said that Mrs Shaw was to have her pearls when she died, but I couldn't find them. My mother had a lot of strange hiding places for her valuables because of burglars. It took me ages to find her rings, camouflaged in a box of safety pins which blended in with the platinum admirably. When I finally found the pearls, by accident in a tangle of old worthless beads I had put aside to get rid of, it was too late: as was everything else.

POSTSCRIPT

The writers' group is getting to be some sort of religion these days.

Last week I read what I had written on the subject of a guilty conscience and brought to light my feelings of having let dear Pauline Shaw down towards the end of her life and just after. The group gave me absolution in their usual supportive way, but there was still the matter of a penance and a few Hail Marys wouldn't do it.

I had to bridge the gap of years since the funeral and get in touch with the family. So one evening after a couple of whiskies I got out my trusty phone directory. I was pretty sure the eldest son, Philip, who was in the building trade, would still be living in Kempston and as I didn't remember the married names of the two daughters it seemed good to start with him. The number was easily found, to my shame, and a few minutes later I found myself talking to his grown-up daughter who seemed to remember all about me and my family and to be very happy to hear from me: as simple as that. I explained how bad I had felt and how the time of silence had lengthened and inertia set in. I mentioned the pearls and how they were now found. She said, somewhat incomprehensibly to me, that they had been afraid I was cross with them. I assured her this was not so and we rang off with mutual good wishes as her father was not in. About three or four minutes after I put the phone down it rang again. It was the eldest daughter Mandy, my special friend, sounding exactly like her old self and calling me Gilly, which doesn't happen so much these days. She asked if she could come and see me on the Sunday evening and I joyfully agreed.

When she arrived, looking very like her mother and beaming all over her face, we just hugged each other very hard. I'd forgotten how small she was – also like her mum. I said would she like a cup of coffee and she said, "Sit down, I'll get it." Which she did very efficiently, seeming to know where everything was kept and we repaired to the withdrawing room for a happy, uninhibited chatter.

It appeared that they had been blaming themselves for not letting me know the date and time of the funeral, and when I said that I should have looked in the paper she said,

"Gilly, you're family, of course you should have been rung up." It transpired that her sister, Wendy, had been charged with this task and said that she had done so. They didn't realise at the time how close poor Wendy was to a nervous breakdown – three weeks later she was in Weller Wing, the collapse no doubt hastened by the death of her mother. I think she really believed she had rung me. It appears the family sat at home before the funeral waiting for me to appear and demanding of Wendy was she sure I hadn't required a lift.

"No", said Wendy "She said she would make her own way".

Finally they had to leave, still looking for me in the church, and afterwards when people went back for tea. The family were all devastated by how quickly Pauline had deteriorated – she had initially gone into hospital with dehydration. Afterwards all her organs seemed to fail rapidly and I put forward to Mandy the idea that she was simply worn out. She said that after her mum stopped working she had seemed to give up.

"I think she thought she wasn't needed anymore." This made me feel very sad but I was done with feeling guilty for something that is all over now and has been so counter-productive. I don't know how Pauline could have felt that; she was so much the king-pin of the family and their disintegration after her funeral proved that. But I think for her, like my father, it was essential to be practical and above all, active in caring for her family and it was the lack of mobility that got her. It wasn't enough to love and be loved: she had to serve.

Mandy told me very simply and touchingly of her own grief and of Wendy's troubles and it was obvious why they had none of them got in touch with me then. It was up to me to do that and I am sorry it has been several years too late. But Pauline had created a solid happy family at the core and this has stood them in good stead. Wendy's marriage failed but she is living in the same road as her sister and her grown up children are living in Kempston and see her often. Their father, Terry, is now living in St John's Almshouses in Kempston and is frail, but still inclined to like a nice fry-up. He apparently comes over to North Wing for a blood test now and then and has asked if he may call in on me. I was touched that Mandy had instantly rung her half-sister Jean in Southport to tell her of my re-emergence and bore messages of good will from her. There were also greetings from the erring Wendy. I handed over the pearls to Mandy and also some pretty beads of my mother's for her daughter Samantha who is now thirteen and obviously a source of great pride and comfort to her mother. Mandy and I said we would meet again soon and I know we will. It was so easy talking to her and we have so many memories in common. It amused me that she immediately started to look after me as her mother had always done.

So there we are. Penance completed. And how silly do I feel! It has all been the result of a sort of moral inertia. All I had to do was pick up the phone and the thing was done. But it needed the catharsis of writing it all down, and a couple of whiskies of course!

CHRISTMAS

Christmas! A word that brings a warmth to my heart immediately, though to some I know it merely brings a sinking feeling to the stomach.: the lonely, those with unhappy memories past and present. This year will be the seventieth Christmas I have lived through and I realise how lucky I have been to have retained the happy feeling it gives me. If the Ghost of Christmas Past appeared to me this year, where would he take me?

The childhood Christmases I remember were all passed in time of war when austerity and the absence of my father in the army seemed likely to cast a shadow on them. But our family, grandparents, aunts, uncles and cousins simply love celebrating and we like nothing better than to do it all together, so there were plenty of people to help cut out the paper chains and assist the fairies to decorate the tree and to read and respond to the hopeful notes left for Father Christmas in the empty fire grates. There were the fur gloves magicked from grandfather's mysterious pockets so that we would be warm when we went carol singing up and down the street with a collector's tin for the waifs and strays, looking probably much like them ourselves. The Ghost might take me to the special Christmas in 1944 when the allies had reached Paris and my father sent me my beautiful French doll, Bernadette, who arrived unbelievably on Christmas Eve. But always the anticipation was the best part of Christmas, so he might transport me to the home of Alice and Archie, who worked for my grandparents and where my mother left me early one Christmas Eve when I was quite young while she went about her adult business. They spoiled me dreadfully and I was plied with food and drink, but what I still remember to this day is how I sat there in a blissful state of suspense, content to wait for Christmas Day to arrive in the absolute assurance that there was real magic all around me. I could see it sparkling in the air and I could hear the sound of tiny bells. For once not surrounded by my noisy family, I had drawn all the anticipating excitement into me and somehow converted it into a feeling of peace and security. The true spirit of Christmas? Perhaps – but with somewhat pagan roots.

Much as I loved my mother I especially valued time spent with the father I had missed so much in my earlier years, just the two of us in our own special world. So my friendly Ghost would not neglect to drop in on us on one of our Christmas Eve car journeys where we traditionally took flowers to both sets of grandparents in Bedford and Kempston cemeteries and went to visit my uncle, Flick's father, whose birthday it was, and then his sister-in-law down the road where my extravagant praise of her exceeding good mince pies was rewarded by more that my fair share of them. My understanding mother would be at home stuffing the turkey and listening to carols from King's College Cambridge.

So many happy Christmases were spent at home that it was not until I was twenty two and working at Canterbury rep that I ever had Christmas apart from my parents. Being in the pantomime I had really no time or energy to go home for one day and I remember the guilty pleasure of a pub-crawl with my dear friend Jean on the Christmas Eve and a hotel lunch the next day. It seemed strange and different. The following year though, when I was still at Canterbury, my parents stayed in the house of one of our playgoers who had gone away for the festivities and they brought the whole Christmas with them. They did the same later on at Cheltenham where we had an exciting time on Christmas Day when Josephine Tewson had really bad toothache and we persuaded a local dentist to open up his surgery for her after lunch. I heard some years later that she had married a dentist, but I don't know if it was the same one! My parents just managed to get home in that year of 1962 / 63 before the big freeze when the snow was piled so high we were cut right off in the Cotswolds.

So many scenes would flicker by me as old Christmas Past did his thing: Christmases in Yorkshire, when I was first married, with my husband's family, spent chiefly in a variety of pubs; Christmases in Southwold where tradition ruled and magic was re-discovered through my young children; the excitement of myself being Santa Claus whose existence I had stoutly defended for so long in my childhood; my daughter in her early teens, taking over the choosing and decorating of the tree in a very superior way, foreshadowing her talents for stage costume and décor; my son's wishing to spend his first Christmas away from us alone with his girl-friend. So many traditions built up in the family over the years. My father always insisted that before we eat at Christmas lunch we raise our glasses and toast absent friends and those who were permanently separated from us. I remember the year after his death in October, when he became one of those toasted and the year in my mother's last illness when my daughter put fairy lights all round her Grandmother's bedroom. Then, among my daughter's friends, the more recent tradition of attempting to throw a Brussel-sprout straight into her open mouth. Her father instigated this one year and everyone failed, amidst much hilarity, until her new boyfriend called in and did it in one. It was obvious they were made for each other.

And I'm sure I would be taken back to the year of my pregnancy with that same daughter when I had been in hospital since the beginning of December because of a condition called placenta previa. They let me out for two days at Christmas, provided I did absolutely nothing but sit still, and my parents brought food and drink up to our London flat, so that their car would be available in case of trouble. And then, early on Boxing Day morning I began to bleed, and the car wouldn't start, and the hospital sent an ambulance and the ambulance men had terrible difficulty getting my large bulk down the stairs in a carrying chair. I remember being wheeled on a trolley looking up at lights and decorations, and then spending thirty hours on a hard bed in a labour ward, trying not to give birth as it was too early. Fortunately, I succeeded and she arrived by caesarean section late in February.

By this time the Ghost and I would be utterly exhausted and he would disappear after offering me an admonitory humbug and promising a visit from his two companions later. Whatever Christmas Future shows me – and I am sometimes fearful because I have had more than my share of good fortune and happiness – nothing can wipe out the past and its memories.

Merry Christmas – and God bless us, every one.

LaVergne, TN USA
04 December 2009
166023LV00005B/194/P